Puppy
Play
THE APP
JP Sayle

Other Books

Standalone
When Fake Changed Everything
Christmas beyond Christmas
The Elves and the Bondage Daddy (Grim and Sinister Delights Book 5)

Series
The Potters Creek Series
A Christmas Wish (book one)

The App Series
The App: Daddy kink (book one)
The App: Littles (book two)
The App: Puppy play (book three)

The Flamingo Bar Series
Always More (book one)
The Little Side of Me (book two)
3 is the magic number (book three) - **Feb 2021**

La Trattoria Di Amore Series
Puzzle Pieces (book one)
Dominated but not Subdued (book two)

The Playroom Series
Mine, Body and Soul: Part One
Mine, Body and Soul: Part Two
Mine, Body and Soul: Part Three
Ferron's Journey: Damaged Part One (book four)
Ferron's Journey: Hidden Part Two (book five)
Ferron's Journey: Revelation Part Three (book six)
Mine, Body and Soul Trilogy
Ferron's Journey Trilogy

Dark River Stone Collective Series
The light beneath the dark

The Billionaire Playground Series
Property of a Billionaire (Book one)
Reluctant Billionaire (Book two)

The Manx Cat Guardians Series
Where it all Began: Origins (Book 1)
Seeing Beyond the Scars (Book 2)
Destiny Collides Past and Present (Book 3)
Searching for a Soul to Love (Book 4)
The 12 Disasters of Christmas (Book 5)
Laws of Attraction (Book 6)
The Teacher's Boy (Book 7)
Boxset

Audio Books

Mine, Body and Soul, Part One: The Playroom Series

Mine, Body and Soul, Part Two: The Playroom Series

Mine, Body and Soul, Part Three: The Playroom Series

Daddy Kink: The App (book one)

Always More: The Flamingo Bar (book one)

When Fake Changed Everything

Ferron's Journey: Damaged Part One

Book Family Tree

Sawyer — (Waiter in LTDA, partner Boyd)—Main Character The App: Littles (book 2) The Little Side of Me, (book 2) The Flamingo Bar. In The App: Daddy Kink, (book 1), La Trattoria Di Amore Series book 1 &2, The Playroom Series books 1-6.

Boyd — (Construction Owner, partner Sawyer)—Main Character The App: Littles (book 2) The Little Side of Me, (book 2) The Flamingo Bar. In Mine, Body and Soul Trilogy: The Playroom Series, The Playroom Series books 1-6.

Isaac — (Bar Manager of The Playroom, Ferron's partner)— Main Character Ferron's Journey Part One: Damaged, (Book 4), Ferron's Journey Part Two: Hidden (Book 5) Ferron's Journey Part Three: Revelation, (Book 6) The Playroom Series. In Dominated but not Subdued: La Trattoria Di Amore Series (book 2), Mine, Body and Soul: The Playroom Series books 1-3. The App series 1-3, The Flamingo Bar Series 1-3.

Ferron — (Bartender in The Playroom, Isaac's partner)— Main Character Ferron's Journey Part One: Damaged, (Book 4), Ferron's Journey Part Two: Hidden (Book 5) Ferron's Journey Part Three: Revelation, (Book 6) The Playroom Series. In La Trattoria Di Amore series book 1&2, Mine, Body and Soul: The Playroom Series books 1-3. The App series 1-3, The Flamingo Bar Series 1-3.

Scott — (Waiter in LTDA, partner Luke)—Main Character The App: Daddy Kink, Always More, Flamingo Bar Series. In La Trattoria Di Amore Series (book 1&2), The Playroom Series books 1-6. The App series 2-3, The Flamingo Bar Series 2-3.

Luke — (Hotel Manager)—Main Character in The App: Daddy Kink, Always More, The Flamingo bar, (book 1). In The Manx Cat Guardians Series, (book 6 & 7), Property of a Billionaire, (book one) Billionaire's Playground.

Adam — (Floor Manager of LTDA, partner Carl)—Main Character Dominated but not Subdued: La Trattoria Di Amore, (book 2). In La trattoria Di Amore book 1, The Playroom Series books 1-6. The App series 1-3, The Flamingo Bar Series 1-3. Billionaire's Playground

Carl — (Head Chef of LTDA and Co-owner of The Playroom, partner Adam)—Main Character Dominated but not Subdued: La Trattoria Di Amore, (book 2). In La Trattoria Di Amore Series (book 1),Mine, Body and Soul Trilogy, The App: Daddy Kink (book 1)

Nathan — (Co-owner of The Playroom, partner Lenny)— Main Character Mine, Body and Soul Trilogy, Playroom Series books 1-3. In The Playroom series books 4-6, La Trattoria Di Amore Series (book 1 & 2), The App series 1-3, The Flamingo Bar Series 1-3.

Lenny — (Trainee Chef of LTDA, partner Nathan)—Main Character Mine, Body and Soul Trilogy, Playroom Series books 1-3. In The Playroom series books 4-6, La Trattoria Di Amore Series (book 1 & 2), The App series 1-3, The Flamingo Bar Series 1-3.

Bailey — (Ex Army Sergeant, partner Sam and Jake)—Main Character The App: Puppy Play (book 3) The App Series, 3 Is the Magic Number, (Book 3) The Flamingo Bar Series. In Part Three Mine Body and Soul: The Playroom Series, Ferron's Journey Part Two: Hidden & Part Three: Revelation, The Playroom Series (Books 5 & 6)

Jake — (Architect, partner Sam and Bailey)— Main Character The App: Puppy Play (book 3) The App Series, 3 Is the Magic Number, (Book 3) The Flamingo Bar Series. In The Playroom Series books 1-6.

Sam — (Bar Manager Flamingo Bar, partner Jake and Bailey)— Main Character The App: Puppy Play (book 3) The App Series, 3 Is the Magic Number, (Book 3) The Flamingo Bar Series. In The Playroom Series books 5&6, The Flamingo Bar Series book 2, The App Series book 2.

Brett — (Psychologist, partner to Guy)—Main Character Reluctant Billionaire, (book 2) Billionaire's Playground. In Billionaire's Playground (book 1), The Flamingo Bar, book 1.

Guy— (Student, partner to Guy)—Main Character Reluctant Billionaire, (book 2) Billionaire's

Playground. In Billionaire's Playground (book 1), The Flamingo Bar, book 1.

Griffin — (Tycoon, partner to Charlie)—Main Character Property of a Billionaire. In The Flamingo Bar Series, book 1, Billionaire's Playground Series book 2.

Charlie — (Student, partner to Griffin)—Main Character Property of a Billionaire. In The Flamingo Bar Series, book 1, Billionaire's Playground Series book 2.

Richie — (Office assistant LTDA, partner Seb)—Main Character La Trattoria Di Amore Series (book 1). In La Trattoria Di Amore, (book 2), In The Playroom series books 1-6, The App series 1-3.

Sebastian — (Co-owner of LTDA restaurants with Carl, partner Richie)—Main Character La Trattoria Di Amore Series (book 1). In La Trattoria Di Amore, (book 2), Mine, Body and Soul Trilogy, The App: Daddy Kink (book 1), The Manx Cat Guardians (book 7)

Theo — (Waiter in LTDA)—La Trattoria Di Amore Series (book 1&2), Mine, Body and Soul Trilogy: The Playroom Series. Ferron's Journey Part One: Damaged, The Playroom Series (book 4), The Flamingo Bar (book 3), The App Series, book 2.

Can an app be what Sam needs to heal his broken heart and overcome his fears after having his lower leg amputated?

After being medically discharged from the army, Sam Villard applies for a job as bar manager at the Flamingo Bar. His hopes of starting a new life flourish when he downloads The App and he meets Jake Alexander, a Dom.

What Sam was not expecting was to find the one man he'd offered his heart to, only to be rejected, living under Jake's roof, Bailey Renfrew. Is Jake the answer to healing past hurts, or will old wounds work to destroy Sam's burgeoning hope?

The App: Puppy Play is an MMM gay romance with a young Dom who knows what he wants: Sam and Bailey. This is the third book in The App Series and can be read as a stand-alone. The conclusion to Sam, Bailey, and Jake's story can be found in 3 is the Magic Number (book 3) The Flamingo Bar Series.

Thank you to Hannah for her insistence that Bailey get his story. To Mandy, Julie, Tina, Abbie and Guy, for your support, comments and feedback, they are, as always invaluable.

PROLOGUE

SAM

The pain that shot through my right leg left me panting. I fought to ride through the gut-wrenching nausea that always followed when I stupidly decided that moving was a good idea. It had been seven weeks since they'd removed the piece of shrapnel that had lodged in my shin bone when Dino, one of the squaddies I'd been out on patrol with, had unwittingly stepped on a landmine. Seven weeks of searing pain every time I moved.

I shut my eyes to block out the images, scents, and sounds of Dino being blown to pieces while several of the other guys and I sustained shrapnel wounds. It was supposed to have been a routine patrol, and the area had allegedly been swept for mines. The intel hadn't been correct though, and Dino had paid for it with his life. A wave of grief crashed over me and I sucked in a sharp breath, while my hands clenched the bedsheet.

Dino and I had been buddies from the outset. He'd had a quirky sense of humour and wasn't offended by the fact I was openly gay. I was gutted that I'd missed his funeral, but I'd been too out of it after my first surgery. I ended up having a second surgery to attempt to save my lower limb after infection got into the bone. It turned out that it was resistant to the antibiotics, and I now had osteomyelitis. The surgeons had done their best, but with the antibiotics not working, they'd come by two days ago to talk options for the next step.

Step, that was a joke!

My heart thudded against my ribs.

Amputation, holy fuck. They were gonna cut off my lower leg! A band of tightness I'd become familiar with over the last two days worked to stop me taking another breath.

Breathe, goddammit.

It didn't matter how many times I'd thought it or said it aloud, it was still shocking to comprehend what that was going to mean to me, to my life, to what it was going to be like once I was medically discharged from the army. They'd said it wasn't a foregone conclusion, but I knew better. The army had been my life since I was twenty, and I have no family to speak of, having spent my youth in foster care. The army had been my family. What did I have if not that? The answer was easy, nothing. The thought left me feeling as if I were floating at sea with nothing to cling to, no one to help, no one to love me and tell me it was going to be all right.

Dino lost his life; all you're losing is a small part of you!

A sob tore at my throat, then air hissed through my clenched teeth as the door opened. My heart sank. *Why now? Why did he have to show up now?*

I swiped at my damp eyes and relaxed against the bed, willing my body to behave in front of the one man I didn't want to show weakness.

"Sarge, this is a surprise." My voice hitched with the effort to keep control.

His dark brows rose. His coal black eyes swept over me and my heart cinched in my chest at the look that crossed over his face that he refused to acknowledge. The fucker loved me, he did. *It's not enough, you're not enough.*

Coldness seeped into my body as I defiantly met his gaze.

I'd first encountered him when he'd been assigned as my Sergeant in the army. For me, it had been lust at first sight. That had been ten years earlier, and my feelings had grown for him, only he'd made sure to keep his distance, putting the army barriers between us.

Why couldn't I move on and find someone else? I scrutinised him. His hair was cropped short and the black held a lot more silver than when we'd first met. There were more lines around his coal black eyes. His face was ruggedly handsome, and age sat well on him. His army greens always appeared to be stretched to capacity around his solid barrel chest, muscular arms, and thick tree-trunk legs. When I looked at him, I had the urge to go and crawl into his lap and be...petted.

Everything about him ticked all my kinky arse boxes, and that was before I'd got to know his intelligent mind, caring nature, and strong sense of right and wrong.

"—didn't you contact me?" His voice held a hint of hurt and pulled me from my perusal.

Not sure what I'd missed, I shrugged. "I'm no longer under your command, Sarge. You made it perfectly clear the last time we spoke that…" I trailed off, recalling the hurt at his rejection.

I rubbed at my face, hoping to dispel the memory of his closed expression after I'd declared my feelings for him.

"I'm sorry," he stated in a rough voice as he came closer, his hand reaching out before it fell back to his side.

Unsure if he were apologising for rejecting me or for me being in the hospital, I remained silent, waiting to see if he'd have the courage to say more.

The seconds stretched, along with my nerves, and I barely resisted the urge to move. It was the certainty that I'd never be able to hide the pain that kept me still.

He gave a heartfelt sigh and took the seat next to my bed. The plastic chair creaked under his weight. His nose twitched, and I prayed it wasn't because of the scent of my decaying leg. I wasn't sure if the room stank or not. I'd got so used to the smell, it was hard to tell sometimes. They'd moved me into the small room on my own due to what was happening later today. I was grateful for the privacy because I wasn't at all sure how I was going to react to waking with half my leg missing.

His gaze fell to the bed sheet covering my lower half, and I flushed.

"I came to see how you are." He paused and licked his lips before his gaze returned to mine. "I also wanted to let you know that I'm being discharged from the army next week."

There was a depth of sadness and regret in his dark eyes, and I was left speechless. The army had been his life and he'd never even hinted that he'd give it up. What had changed? "Did something happen?"

"It's just time...I'm forty-six, and there has to be more to life than this." His arms lifted to encompass the white box-room in the army base hospital. I was clearly missing something, but his face became unreadable and the 'mind your own business' sign over his head couldn't be missed. I'd seen it too many times to misunderstand, he didn't want to talk to me.

"You didn't answer my question, how are you?" His gaze yet again drifted down to my legs. It was hard to miss that my right leg was covered in a bulky dressing.

"I'm fine." I lied through my teeth and gave him a fake cheery smile. "A few more days and maybe they'll release me, and then I'll be on the dreaded restricted duty."

Lines appeared to deepen around his eyes and mouth as he gave me a speculative look. "How are you coping with Dino's death?" he asked ever so gently, reminding me why he was good at his job. He cared.

My hands trembled and I clenched the sheet. "Gutted, to be truthful. I never got to say goodbye to him." A lone tear slid down my cheek and I blinked to clear my vision. "I've an appointment to see someone to talk about it." I didn't add that my new sergeant had insisted, knowing I was about to lose a limb. It was nice someone cared about where my head was at, even if it was only because they were paid to make sure I didn't lose it.

He nodded. "That's good." He seemed to struggle to find anything more to say to me and I got it. After I'd told him I love him and he'd rejected me, we'd avoided each other until I'd deployed several months ago. We'd not seen or spoken since, and what had once been an easy relationship was now besieged by uncomfortable silences.

A nurse bustled into the room and, taking in Sarge's rank, stood to attention. "Sergeant, I'm sorry, but I'm going to have to ask you to leave as we need—"

Scared she was about to say more than I wanted her to, I jumped in. "He's just leaving."

Her face lost a little of its colour at my rudeness, but Bailey stood. "I'll leave you to it." His posture was stiff and his face unreadable as he glanced between me and the nurse before he shook his head. His lips pinched together as if he were about to say something then thought better of it. A flash of sadness broke through a crack in his defences, I was sure of it, but before I could look closer, he was gone.

The silence was deafening as my heart wept for the one thing it couldn't have.

"That was nice of the sergeant to come and wish you well for your surgery."

Was it? It didn't feel like it when my insides felt scraped raw. The nurse continued to chat as she took my blood pressure, pulse, and temperature. And I didn't dissuade her of the notion as she got me ready to go to theatre. Why would I? There had been nothing between us, and now there never could be.

Bailey hadn't wanted me whole, there was no way he'd want me after the surgery. Tears clogged my throat and I swallowed them back, sniffling.

Fuck it! Fuck it! Fuck it!

It was time to move on and accept that the love I hungered after wasn't for me.

Let's see how that works for you when it's never changed in years!

I heaved a sigh and shut my eyes. *I can change, I can!*

CHAPTER ONE

SAM

I exited the taxi carefully, watching for any potholes that could cause me to embarrass myself by going arse over tit. The months of recovery and getting used to wearing a prosthetic had been gruelling, but as I stood outside the huge, converted warehouse, I got a sense of pride at having accomplished so much in such a short time.

Yes, there were still bad days that could be soul-destroying, but they were getting fewer and fewer. So much so, that when I'd seen the ad for the bar manager's position at The Flamingo Bar, I'd taken it as a sign that I was ready to face the world properly. That it was also a kink bar spoke to a part of me I'd tucked to one side while I'd been working on figuring out who I was now. The old me was a full-throttle kind of guy, the new me had to think carefully about logistics and capabilities.

A little of the happiness I'd felt at getting an interview, waned. Would I be judged because I was different?

You won't find out standing on the curb.

I shifted my weight, ensuring I was balanced before pulling out my phone and searching for the instructions on how to access the bar. The email with the offer of an interview had mentioned I'd need to go through the underground car park. I searched the busy street and spotted the sign that indicated the underground parking entrance was further down from where I stood.

My stomach jittered. Should I have told them about my leg?

Stop second guessing yourself and go in.

I shrugged off the worry, and headed in the direction the sign indicated, walking with a slightly awkward gait as I worked to tighten my core muscles and roll my hips. It had taken an age to understand that holding everything tight at my core would make it easier to keep my balance. The eight pack I now sported from the exercise regime my physio had given me, didn't hurt my ego at all as long as I chose to ignore what was lacking further down.

In the garage, I glanced about then walked towards the lift, humming in approval. If this was the access to the second floor, then it would offer privacy to members who preferred to keep their kink under the radar.

As I got out of the lift, I was met with a wall of noise. The sounds of workmen came from everywhere. The place looked nowhere near ready. There was debris everywhere I looked. *Fuck's sake!*

I worked to keep the worry off my face at how I was going to manage to cross the room without being obvious about my disability. The application had asked about disabilities, and I'd sweated over admitting mine for fear they wouldn't even give me an interview.

Bile burned the back of my throat, and as I swallowed, I searched for someone that looked in charge. My pulse skipped a beat as I noticed the two men stood over by the bar having a conversation. Instantly recognising the tall blond dude, I cursed under my breath. Nathan! Shit, was he the Nathan that was part owner of the bar and club downstairs? It had to be! Why hadn't I put two and two together?

The big bear stood next to him, looking a tad uncomfortable at whatever Nathan was saying, I didn't recognise, but he gave off an air of someone that had been in the forces. When neither man seemed to be aware of my presence, and time ticked by, I lifted my arm to catch their attention, not wanting them to think I'd arrived late.

"Hey, there's a dude standing by the door, trying to get your attention," shouted a guy as he passed by Nathan and the other man, lugging a toolbox.

Nathan's attention shifted immediately towards me, and I realised my error. *Why didn't you walk to them first?*

When the other guy's head tilted to one side, I intuitively knew he was taking in my odd gait as I walked towards them. Paying him no attention, or at least trying not to, I scrutinised the floor, carefully navigating around the various objects scattered across it.

When my prosthetic leg caught on a bit of debris, I quickly righted myself but heat flooded my face. Feelings of defiance surfaced, and when the guy stood next to Nathan released a noisy breath, I met his gaze square on.

As I stopped in front of both men, it struck me just how big they were. Although I was six foot, I was lean, with a well-developed chest from all the workouts. These guys were built like Hulk Hogan.

Nathan held out his hand. "I'm Nathan, this is Isaac, the bar manager from The Playroom."

"I'm Sam Villard, thanks for meeting me." I took Nathan's large hand and shook it before offering my hand to Isaac. "Nice to meet you both."

My gaze moved between both men, assessing their reaction to me before I turned my attention to the half-finished room.

"Have we met before?" Nathan asked.

I reluctantly looked back at him. "Once. You came to say goodbye to Sarge, and I was just leaving his office." I was dismayed at the emotion I could hear in my voice, but there was little I could do about it.

Nathan's large hand came up, and before I realised his intention, he patted me on the shoulder with some force. I silently cursed as I wobbled slightly before Isaac lurched forward to steady me, making my humiliation complete.

I met Isaac's gaze. "I'm fine," I ground out, sounding ungrateful for the help as I pushed at his hands.

It took a second before he released my arm and stepped back. "I'm sure you are, but from one comrade to another, we don't leave a man to struggle."

Nathan's brow rose and he wore a nonplussed expression. He clearly hadn't worked out the reason for my lack of balance. I swallowed the sigh when Isaac, who clearly got what was up with me, folded his arms and said nothing.

"What am I missing here?" Nathan glanced between us before his gaze settled on me.

"I've got a prosthetic leg that I'm still getting used to. But it won't prevent me from doing the job," I said in a defensive tone, as yet more heat flooded my face and I forced myself to meet Nathan's gaze.

"I'm sure it wouldn't," Nathan stated, "but I'd like to point out that you haven't been interviewed yet."

Isaac's Adam's apple bobbed several times as his lips twitched, and I gave Nathan a contrite look. "Yeah, sorry. I'm just trying to figure things out."

Nathan was more careful when he placed his hand on my shoulder the second time, his face showing compassion. "If you wanna talk about it, I'm a good listener. We all have our scars to bear." Nathan's voice thickened, but his face displayed a meaning I couldn't even begin to grasp as he stared at me.

"Thanks." I rasped past my dry throat. Blinking rapidly and feeling totally flustered, I glanced about, keeping my gaze away from both men so they couldn't see I was about two seconds away from blubbering. It had been far too long since anyone had shown me even a smidgen of care. "You gonna show me around?"

"Come on then," Nathan answered.

The time flew, and after saying goodbye, I walked to the lift breathing a sigh of relief. After the first hour, a good feeling had started to grow from the questions Nathan asked while we'd toured the building. When I could easily answer his questions, I'd found myself relaxing and envisioning myself running the bar.

The disability pension from the army was okay, but it wasn't enough to live on in London. The room I rented currently was a shithole, but it would do until I got a job. The money Nathan was offering would allow me to live a lot more comfortably, even if the hours might be hard going to start with.

I worried my lip between my teeth as I waited for my Uber to arrive.

After that initial little mishap, I'd been sure-footed and had even shown off my titanium leg, hoping to show I'd adapted. The question was, did I have the stamina needed to do the job?

You haven't got it yet.

Yet!

Chapter Two

Jake

The headache brewing behind my eyes showed all the signs of turning into a migraine if I didn't stop what I was doing and take a break. Placing my trusted Staedtler Mars Matic pen, which I'd had for nearly twenty years, next to the drawings I'd been working on, I groaned as I sat back. All the muscles in my back protested at once, not enjoying being moved from the bent over position I'd been in for the last six hours.

I wearily eyed the clock sat on the far wall and huffed out a breath. How had it got to one a.m. and I'd not noticed...again?

There is no one to tell you to stop, that's why.

It had been far too long since I'd had a reason to stop working to go and...what?

Fuck knows! It's not like you know what you want.

First it was a sub, then it was a boy, then it was...Bailey.

Nathan's request to rent out my spare room to his old sergeant had given me something I hadn't expected; a man who challenged my Dom persona. My eyes drifted shut as Bailey's face appeared in front of my eyelids. Our first meeting had been a somewhat tense introduction, to say the least. My tired brain was no defence against the memories as they flooded my head and took me back.

"This is turning into a bigger job than I anticipated," Boyd complained, scowling at me.

"Hey, it's not my fault this bozo decided to change the egress and access to accommodate a restaurant," I stated more than a little aggressively to Boyd, pointing my thumb in Nathan's direction.

"Will you two stop it? You're giving me a headache with all your bitching. Christ! I don't know what's worse, listening to you two, or thinking about how Carl is going to react when you explain to him that he can't have everything he wants." Nathan sounded utterly frustrated.

Although my initial idea to move a wall worked for some aspects, it, unfortunately, didn't work when it came to the stability of the building structure or the permits that were needed.

"Hell no, I ain't explaining shit to Carl," Boyd ground out, his jaw flexing as his gaze narrowed on me. "You'll have to do it. It's your bloody stupid ideas that got us into this mess in the first place."

"Who the fuck do you think you're talking to?" I all but growled, my inner Dom coming to the fore as Boyd strode towards me, getting in my face.

I bristled as Boyd tried to drill a hole in my chest with his finger, sneering. "You, you arsehole! Does it look like there's another arsehole in the vicinity?"

There was a blur of movement and a resounding thud that vibrated through my shoes, *followed by a large plume of dust that choked me as Nathan let out a curse.*

"What the fuck, Bailey?" Nathan asked, his face aghast.

Bailey? Is this who is going to be renting my spare room? My brow arched as the man stood over a prone Boyd, his broad back towards me as if he were shielding me. The scent of his woodsy aftershave greeted my nose as I inhaled greedily at the sight of the muscular body straining against his jacket.

Everyone seemed to pause to re-group while Boyd, his face the colour of a ripe tomato and his chest heaving, struggled to get up off the dirty floor. Nathan moved first to offer his hand to help him up.

What the fuck had just happened? Wasn't Bailey supposed to be a submissive? Why was he acting like my Dom? Did he think I needed protecting?

"I think we need to cool things down. I'm not sure what the fuck just happened here, but it fucking stops now," Nathan stated firmly.

Boyd nodded stiffly before he glanced at me. "I'm sorry I lost my cool like that. I was maybe a little frustrated with the number of things that have gone wrong today. I shouldn't have taken it out on you." He sounded contrite as he brushed his hands down his dirty jeans, removing some of the dirt.

Bailey muttered under his breath, "Too fucking right you shouldn't," but it was loud enough for me to hear. Unfortunately, I couldn't see his face as he still stood with his back towards me.

I found myself saying, "It's cool, things just got a little heated and out of control. I'm sorry, Boyd, if I was a dick." I gave him a half-smile and then stepped towards the hand he held out.

A low growl made both me and Boyd freeze. The questions returned. Was Bailey a Dom? Had I missed something when Nathan had spoken about him?

Nathan took hold of Bailey's arm, and in a lowered voice I could only just hear, said, "I'm not sure what's going on with you, but ease off, Sarge. You're frightening the natives."

Bailey appeared to tense for a second before he acquiesced and took a step to the side. It was only then that I saw his face. His grey eyes appeared silver with whatever emotions he was feeling. His short-cropped hair showed off high cheekbones that complimented his square jaw and full lips. I felt a tug of arousal low in my stomach.

Boyd eyed Bailey warily as he took the hand I still held out and released it after a couple of shakes. "Well, I've got shit to do. Jake, can you get the new plans to me so I can pass them by the building inspector?"

I nodded. "Yeah, I'll work on them tonight and send them to you tomorrow."

With that, Boyd walked off, his posture stiff, not once looking back to where we all stood in an uncomfortable silence. I remained silent, unsure of what to say. Bailey seemed disinclined to say anything as I stared at him. The arousal I'd felt turned into an unexpected flutter in my chest at him very slowly lowering his gaze in submission. But I'd seen something else far more worrying; sadness.

I didn't get a chance to dwell on it as Nathan broke the weird tension between us. "Bailey Renfrew, I'd like you to meet Jake Alexander, your new...landlord." He paused, looking between us, then a phone buzzed, and he dug his hand into his jeans.

Nathan pulled out his phone and glanced at the screen, looking none too pleased as he answered and stepped away from us.

The moment he was out of hearing range, I asked, "Can you explain that behaviour to me, Bailey?"

His gaze remained down while his hands disappeared behind his back. His posture became fully submissive at the tone of my voice. My heart danced against my rib cage, even as I warned myself he'd not be interested in a younger Dom.

"I...I didn't like the way he was acting towards you...Sir." His voice increased in strength, but his gaze remained on the floor, somewhere between us.

The hum of arousal increased. Paying tenant, he's just a paying tenant.

"Do you think I'm weak and need defending?" My voice deepened, and he shuddered.

He nodded, then colour flared across his cheekbones.

That will never do. "Is that so? When was the last time you had a Dom?"

His breath hitched. "It's been a long time."

"Then maybe you've forgotten what it's like to meet a Dom who is more than capable of protecting not only himself, but his...sub."

There was the sound of scraping wood across the floor above my head, and my thoughts returned to the present. I glanced up at the cream ceiling as I rubbed at my throbbing temples. Was Bailey struggling to sleep again?

Bailey had been living with me for three months, and since that weird first meeting, he tried to act like he'd not felt a connection between us. Although, if he was forced to be in the same room as me for any length of time, he struggled to not act submissive towards me. It was gratifying that he felt the need as much as I did, but it messed with my head when it was always accompanied by sadness. It would appear it was why I was up till one in the morning most nights, working to avoid thinking about him and the weird dynamic between us.

All my life, I'd been taught to work towards what I wanted. The only part of my life it had fully worked for me was with architecture. I'd known from the age of seven, when my father had bought me my first miniature drafting table after I'd gone to his office and insisted I needed one, that I wanted to draw. But not just draw, I wanted to create, to leave a legacy the same as my father.

I'd trained and worked hard, taking the grunt work until I'd made partnership in my father's firm at the age of twenty-five. It wasn't because of nepotism, but the strength of my work that spoke for itself. That was eleven years ago, and since then, my designs had won awards and I had more work than ever. I should be ecstatic that I'd succeeded. Fuck, I'd built my own home. I had no mortgage and could easily afford anything I wanted. Then why did I feel empty? When had my life started to leave a sour taste in my mouth?

When you woke up and realised there was more to life than work.

The throbbing increased at my temples and I shut my eyes, hoping I could block out the answer I wasn't ready to face.

CHAPTER THREE

BAILEY

"Why have you been avoiding me, Sarge? It wouldn't be because you don't wanna talk about why you quit the army? Or the fact that in the three months you've been living with Jake, you've not once visited the club to find a Dom. Why is that?" Nathan's face showed concern as he came around the counter that separated the large living space of his apartment.

The sky was bright-blue, and sunlight poured through the large windows behind him as he strolled towards me carrying the two mugs of coffee he'd made. His blond hair was ruffled like he'd run his hands through it several times. His low-slung joggers and plain grey T-shirt showed he had no plans of going anywhere this morning, and my heart sank.

Once he'd placed the mugs down in front of us on the table, he sat down next to me, his expression full of determination. It matched this morning's text, which had been straight to the point.

Get your arse over here and don't give me any bullshit excuses.

I didn't blame him. He'd been pestering me to visit since the impromptu stag party we had back in February for Adam, the now husband of the co-owner of The Playroom, Carl. It wasn't that I didn't want to come and see Nathan, it was more his habit of wheedling information from me that had me avoiding him. A Dom always wanted to take care of a sub in distress, and I was definitely that.

I'd not sought out a new Dom since I'd stupidly fallen in love with someone that was too like me. A part of me felt I'd be betraying Sam if I went with another man.

How can that be when you haven't told him how you feel?

There was no answer to that because it was fucked up. That didn't stop the yearning for a Dom to take me to that place where I could leave the world behind and just feel.

I glanced at Nathan's pensive face. "I'm not good company. I've got a lot going on in my head right now." I offered up a half-truth, but Nathan raised just one brow and sighed. "I don't know where to start," I tagged on lamely.

"At the beginning if it helps. I'm here for you, Sarge, just like you were when I needed support." Nathan laid a warm, comforting hand on my arm, and that simple gesture broke the flood gate.

"I fell in love with a soldier." It came out sounding garbled and I had to take several deep breaths to stop my voice from quivering. "He doesn't know. I never acted on my feelings. You know me, sticking to the rules is how I've managed to keep going. Only, with him, I broke all my own rules."

"How could you have broken your own rules if nothing happened?" Nathan's brow furrowed, but there was sympathy swimming in his eyes.

"He's like me, that's how. He's not a Dom," I whispered mournfully, the grief as real today as it was when I rejected him. It surfaced hard and fast and crushed my heart, leaving me struggling for breath.

"Does he have feelings for you?"

"Yes...he's not a coward like me. He came to see me before he was due to deploy and confessed to how he felt." A strangled sob got stuck in my throat, and Nathan moved to drape an arm over my shaking shoulders.

Long minutes passed as I sobbed, releasing the pain. Pain I'd caused, and then had to carry like a martyr.

"Sam, fuck, he's so brave." I felt Nathan tense, but I put it down to my confession, so I carried on. "Yet my own insecurities have crippled me. He's too much like me. He needs a dominant not a submissive, and I understood his needs because they match my very own perfectly. Did I tell him any of this? Did I? Fuck no. I stood mute while he stood in front of me, declaring his feelings. He left thinking I felt nothing, all because I thought it was for the best." I swiped at my wet cheeks and rested my head on Nathan's shoulder, taking solace from the comfort he was freely giving me, even when I didn't deserve it.

"And what do you feel now?"

The softly spoken question was easy to answer.

Like a coward.

Cowardice had ruled my whole life. Instead of doing what I wanted, I'd done what my father and grandfather had wanted and joined the army. It was their dream, never mine. No, I'd yearned to go to art school, but had I stood up and refused, *no*.

My shoulders slumped, and Nathan's arm tightened around me as a reel of the many things I'd done to please others filtered through my head. I cursed.

"Cowardly," I stated bluntly. When he didn't try to defend me, I said, "I quit the army because my Father died, and I had nobody's expectations to live up to anymore. You'd think I could go and embrace the lifestyle I've wanted more than any career, wouldn't you?"

"But?" Nathan didn't let me hide from the hard truth.

"Is the one thing I've found that allows me to let go and be me, going to be the one thing that fucks up my whole life?" The question hung between us.

When he remained silent, I glanced sideways to look at him. "It is, isn't it?" I stated fatalistically, only then noticing his expression. My brows rose and my stomach rolled over. "Why do you look like you're preparing for a mission?"

"Do you believe in fate?" he asked cryptically, not answering me.

"Right now, I'm not sure what I believe in." It was the truth. I'd lost sight of my life and it had unravelled in front of me. Was my love of BDSM preventing me from living a life where I got to be with the man I wanted? Possibly? But was the peace and joy I found in submission something I could give up and never crave again?

My innards quivered at the very idea. I was fucked no matter how I looked at it, and fate couldn't change that.

"I think you need to pay a visit to the Flamingo Bar and sample some of the new delights that are on offer. You never know what you might find there," he coaxed. I gave an internal sigh when the light of determination in his eyes increased.

"I'll think about it—"

"No, that won't work for me. You've been thinking for months and got nowhere. You're a man of action, you always have been. It's time to face who you are and what you want, no matter how painful that is." Nathan paused, sitting forward to pick up what had to be cold coffee and taking a sip.

Instantly missing the warmth of his body, I sagged against the sofa. Nathan's wince said I was right about the coffee being cold and, a second later, he placed the mug back down with a scowl on his face.

He shifted to face me, his hand reaching out to clasp one of mine. "You know more than anyone how hard it was for me to be open with Lenny. But fuck, it was worth it." His voice was thick with emotion, and the love for Lenny was there for anyone to see.

"I know, but he's a natural sub...I can't be a Dom. I've spent most of my work life being dominant, and it's slowly killing me inside. With the death of my father last year, I felt I was finally free to stop living my life by someone else's expectations." I shuddered at the grief that ran right alongside the resentment I'd not come to terms with. "Anyway, this is all moot because Sam is still serving in the army. He's also sixteen years my junior, besides all the other issues."

When Nathan laughed, I scowled at him. "What the fuck man?"

"I'm sorry, but you and I have way too much in common when it comes to baggage. Age gap issues and different lifestyles being only the tip of the iceberg. Can I ask, have you reached out to...Sam in the last few months?"

The phone in my pocket felt like a lead brick at the obvious answer. "No. I thought it was best for both of us if I kept my distance."

I reached into my pocket, and before I could talk myself out of what I was about to do, I opened the camera roll to find the picture I'd snapped of Sam one day when I'd seen him in the training yard.

He'd been laughing at something one of the guy's he'd been with had said. His whole face was alight with humour as the sun had made his hair gleam with gold threads. I'd found myself reaching for my phone to capture the moment. My cheeks pinked, even as my heart ached to look at his happy face. I'd considered deleting it, but for the life of me, there was no way I could. I gave a humourless chuckle at how I'd saved it in every conceivable place so as not to lose the image, ever.

My fingers clamped around the phone before I offered it to Nathan. "That's him. I'm not sure if you'd left before he was recruited."

Nathan took the phone from my stiff fingers and stared at the screen with a look I couldn't interpret. "I can see why you love him. He's beautiful," he muttered, almost like he was talking to himself.

Then his gaze moved from the screen to me. "Have you ever considered that maybe there is another answer to having everything you w—"

"I've already told you, I can't be a Dom," I ground out, my jaw bunching.

He shook his head and gave me a stern Dom-look that I instantly reacted to. I lowered my gaze and mumbled, "Sorry, Sir." I'd never been attracted to Nathan, but away from work, I'd always shown him respect for who he was.

"Apology accepted." His hand ran over my hair, offering me comfort but nothing more. "If you'd let me finish, I'd have explained that I was thinking about a third. Someone to possibly give both you *and* Sam what you need."

Jake's face sprung to my mind so fast, I blinked to make sure he hadn't suddenly appeared in the room. My cock reacted in a way I'd never have expected, and I swallowed as a flush of heat rode through my body.

Nathan scrutinised me, and the warmth spread into my face. "I'd say by your body's reaction, it might be a solution." A mischievous grin spread over his face. "Care to tell me who you were thinking about when I mentioned a third? Or should I take a wild stab in the dark and say...Jake?"

Why did he have to know me so well? I met his gaze and pointed out the obvious flaw. "It's immaterial when Sam is miles away and Jake...well, I'm sure that's not what he's into."

Nathan fired back, "You've admitted you haven't spoken to Sam in months, and I'd bet my last quid you've been avoiding Jake 'cause of how you've been feeling. All I'm suggesting is give it some thought. In the meantime, you'll come to the Flamingo Bar on Saturday night and live a little."

I left Nathan an hour later, having agreed to meet him and Lenny on Saturday to play gooseberry, but it had got him off my back.

As I walked out into the warm spring weather, I took a deep breath, realising that talking had reduced the heavy weight I'd been lugging around. I felt marginally lighter for the first time in months as I considered Nathan's suggestion. Could introducing a third be the answer, or would it just cause jealousy?

Hold up, as you rightly pointed out to Nathan, Sam isn't even here, and doesn't know you love him.

I heaved a sigh and strode down the packed street towards the tube station.

Fuck, why did life have to be so complicated?

Who the fuck knows!

CHAPTER FOUR

SAM

A trickle of sweat slid down my back as I downloaded the app that Nathan had generously waived the fee for. I stared at my phone screen as the circle of doom whirred around, seemingly taking forever.

There were many benefits to working and managing a place where I got to be a part of the kink world I loved. It really was a dream come true. It did, however, have one major flaw, it was like being diabetic in a sweet shop. Everything around me contained sugar and I couldn't eat anything. That's what it felt like to have no one to play with.

Unfortunately, it highlighted the lack in my own life. I'd not played since I'd had my leg amputated, and it didn't help that I found it difficult to put myself out there with strangers, the huge possibility of rejection constantly hanging over my head.

Then there was the possibility I'd freak out if they touched my stump. Showering and putting cream on had taken some getting used to. The skin could become inflamed with the friction of the cup my stump sat in. I had to examine it daily to ensure I didn't end up with a pressure sore. It was a constant threat, and as I didn't want to lose any more of my leg, I was vigilant about checking it twice a day.

Nathan had got a perching seat for the back of the bar so I could take the weight off my leg. I'd wanted to argue, but after the third consecutive day at work, I'd given in and used it. I'd spent far too many hours after, staring down at my throbbing stump and cursing my own stupidity.

I glanced down at the bare stump, no longer surprised not to see my foot. The scar was a deep purple and lumpy to touch. It sometimes felt like my leg was still there, which had freaked me out on more than one occasion when the phantom pain shot through my non-existent lower limb.

They'd cut below my knee joint with the hope that would be enough. I'd feared initially that they might have had to go higher and amputate above my knee. All the research I'd done predicted that it could be a longer recovery if they had to do another surgery. I'd prayed like a motherfucker, and then some. Someone up there had been listening thankfully because I'd healed with no further signs of the original infection.

After everything I'd been through...*don't think about Bailey, don't do it.*

My throat became clogged as I blinked several times and forcibly focused on the phone in my hand and what I was about to do. *Moving forward remember, you can't go back.*

My heart fluttered with what that meant. Could The App help?

When Ferron and Isaac had talked about The App, I'd been intrigued but felt it was cheeky to get Isaac to ask Nathan for a discount, so I'd left it. Then, the day before, Nathan had mentioned it in passing, and I'd seen it as a golden opportunity to say I was interested in using it. He'd gone off, and I'd thought no more about it until he'd come back with a code for me to use to prevent me being charged.

As I'd been at work and didn't finish until late last night, I'd opted to wait until this morning, knowing I had the day off and could check out what it offered at my leisure.

As soon as the open icon appeared on the screen, I exhaled in a noisy rush and tapped it. I started to read the information, then sighed. I was going to need to fill in quite a bit of information before I could get started. I eyed the coffee I'd made, and my stomach gurgled loudly.

Food first then kink! I chuckled as I got up on one leg and hopped into the tiny kitchen in the one-bedroom apartment I'd moved into from the shared digs I'd been living in. Although the place wasn't big enough to swing a cat in, it was great to have total privacy after the last ten years in the army. Although I'd never minded sharing with others, in fact I'd enjoyed the company most of the time.

As a foster child that nobody wanted, I'd spent a lot of time alone, trying to entertain myself. I can't say the foster families I was placed with didn't try, they did, they were just a little thoughtless.

Was that why I never quite fitted in? *Come on, that's a bit heavy, even for you.*

I finished heating a breakfast burrito, the shop not far from the club made them so good they were almost addictive, and hopped back to sit on the small two-seater sofa I'd bought second-hand. It sagged a little in the middle, but the maroon padded cushions were clean and still had lots of wear in them.

Phone in hand, I munched on my breakfast as I read through everything twice before I dusted off my fingers and started to fill in my details. My eyes were squinting at the tiny screen by the time I got to the point of picking a username.

I glanced at the open bedroom door and visualised the drawer I kept my puppy gear in. The usual little flutter of excitement buzzed to life. The package with my new knee-protectors had arrived two days earlier. The physio had recommended a company that specialized in making and adapting equipment for amputees. I'd contacted them to ask about knee pads. I hadn't explained what they were for, but the guy had been more than helpful. I'd had to send measurements of both knees, and boy, the fit was wonderful. It felt good to be able to slip them on and find I could move more easily over the floor, even without using my right leg. The carpet in the flat wasn't the best to move on, but I'd got a feel for how easy I'd be able to move in a larger space with wooden floors.

They were black to match the leather mask I'd had handcrafted to fit my face. I'd had others, but they'd pinched the skin or felt uncomfortable, which could be distracting, and defeated the purpose of being a puppy. It had taken an age to save until I could afford something custom made, but it had been worth the expense. I now had the mask, collar, lead, and several different tails that were beautifully handcrafted from the softest leather.

The dog collar had my name on, as did the lead, but as yet, I'd never had the courage to offer it to someone. Not with the significance of what it meant to me.

That's because you want to give it to...Bailey.

"I don't need reminding," I muttered to the empty room.

I focused back on what name I should use. Playfulpuppy? I tapped into the box to see if it were already taken. My head tilted, and when it came up as available, I sucked my lower lip between my teeth. Should I use that, or go with something else? I hummed to myself as I went ahead and saved it.

The app produced my landing page, and I was all set to go. With a trembling finger, I scrolled down the list until I got to those seeking a puppy to play with. When I clicked in, my eyes widened at the sheer size of the list of men registered for puppy play. Feeling a little daunted, I started to read.

I wasn't sure how long I'd been reading when I blinked the room into focus, my arse numb and the sun low in the sky. How the hell was I supposed to pick someone?

I stood carefully and rubbed at my numb backside with my free hand as I continued to read. My heart did a fluttery thing, making my finger hesitate to push up the screen to read the next guy's information. I reread the information displayed for: Opentoeverything.

I'm a Dom that is interested in finding someone to build beautiful architecture with. Our structures can be changed and adapted with the right care and attention to detail. There is nothing that can't be overcome.

A tear rolled down my cheek as I gave a heartfelt sigh. Did he really mean that? There was only one way to find out. I blew out a breath and started to type.

Playfulpuppy: *My architecture has been damaged. Are you up for a challenge?*

I read it, and before I could second guess myself, pressed send and shut my eyes the instant it said it was delivered.

Oh fuck.

CHAPTER FIVE

JAKE

My phone buzzed on my desk, but I ignored it for a moment while I finished transferring the dimensions of my hand-drawn design into the computer program I used. I tended to draw all my designs first and I'd never got out of the habit. There were some great computer programs that could do all sorts of fancy designs with 3D and 4D imaging, but I still loved the process of seeing the design come to life on draft paper first.

I breathed out a deep sigh of relief when I finished inputting the information. It was a painstaking process, and I hated to be interrupted when doing it. One wrong hit of a key could have a client thinking we were a bunch of amateurs if you didn't immediately notice a mistake, especially if it threw out all the other dimensions of the plan.

The phone buzzed again, only this time the alert tone indicated that it wasn't a text but a message from The App. My brows rose. When was the last time I'd had anyone message me? I came up blank. Was it because of my updated status? I shrugged. It didn't matter as I'd got fed up with the wannabe subs and boys seeking a Daddy Dom, but had no clue what it was they were actually into.

The App, in essence, was a forum to meet people who were into different kinks and to ask questions. I'd spoken to Nathan extensively about how great the community was that The App had created. The Flamingo Bar had, in part, come about from the many people out there that wouldn't necessarily go to a BDSM club, but who would go to a kink bar more geared to the lighter elements of play.

My pulse missed a beat as I reached for my phone and unlocked the screen to press on The App icon. The message box appeared, and I chuckled at the name **Playfulpuppy**. That was a first for me. I clicked into his profile so I could see the picture he'd used more clearly. A black leather puppy mask covered the top half of his face, leaving his full lips exposed. I stared down at the soulful, deep-blue eyes and felt a stirring of desire deep in my belly.

Had he used a selfie?

I had a moment to wonder what he thought of my picture. My lips twitched at the one I'd chosen of me wearing assless chaps. I'd been told I had a drool worthy backside, so I'd set up my phone to take a selfie of my arse.

Playfulpuppy: *My architecture has been damaged. Are you up to a challenge?*

A buzz of excitement I'd not felt for some time...okay, since I'd first faced off with Bailey all those months ago, thrummed through me. What did he mean by his architecture was damaged? My lips pursed as I typed back.

Opentoeverything: *I've developed a lot of skills over the years and I'm always up for a challenge.*

I hit send and sat back in my office chair. Something told me I wouldn't have to wait long for a response, and I wasn't mistaken. The little dots appeared almost straight away to show that he was responding. A slow smile spread over my lips as I waited to see what he'd say.

Playfulpuppy: *Are you any good at handling a damaged puppy with a sore leg?*

There it was again, the word *damaged*. My eyes narrowed as I responded.

Opentoeverything: *How damaged? Does it count that I'm an animal lover, especially with enthusiastic puppies?*

For some reason, I held my breath waiting for his reply. I hadn't lied about being an animal lover. I'd had a dog all through my childhood. It was only when I'd gone to uni and then to work that I'd given up on the idea of having a pet. It was cruel to leave a dog locked inside alone all day.

As the seconds ticked by and there was no answer, I groaned. Had I pushed too far, asking about the damaged part?

About to put the phone down and go back to work, the writing bubbles appeared, and I was back to holding my breath.

Playfulpuppy: *I've had my right lower leg amputated...*

The air hissed through my teeth as the words punched into my chest. A surge of emotion I wasn't expecting caused my fingers to tremble while I typed back.

Opentoeverything: *There's a story there, and I'd love to hear it if you're up for sharing?*

I stared at what I'd written, and I realised that I did want to know his story. There was something about his honesty and bravery at putting himself out there that drew me. So I hit send and hoped I'd asked the right thing.

Playfulpuppy: *In person or through here?*

It felt like a trick question.

Opentoeverything: *In person works for me.*

My palms started to sweat as he typed back.

Playfulpuppy: *That works for me. When and where do you want to meet? I manage a bar, so I work odd hours, just so you know.*

I'd chosen to work from home today, and had no meetings to attend, so was about finished for the day. Would he think I was too eager if I suggested we meet today?

Opentoeverything: *You must be off today? I've just finished for the day. You want to go out for a bite to eat?*

Playfulpuppy: *I've not eaten since breakfast so that would be a big yes for me. I'm not picky and have no clue as to where to eat in London unless it's fast-food, so I'll leave the place up to you.*

Was it seriously this easy?

Go with it!

I rolled my eyes at myself and searched for somewhere close by that I'd be able to make a last-minute reservation.

I lived just on the outskirts of Notting Hill, having bought an old house that was a crumbling mess. In the end, it had been condemned, but I'd bought it for the land rather than the house, so I'd knocked it down and then spent three years building my dream home. The plot wasn't very big, so I'd built up. The house had four storeys, and I'd created a roof terrace that had a tinted glass ceiling that opened up but offered sufficient privacy when closed. The third floor was open plan and used as a living space. The kitchen took up one end of the room and had a tiny terrace so I could eat alfresco in the summer.

The second floor housed three bedrooms, one of which was my master-suite. The ground floor was where I'd set up my home office, a gym, and a cinema room because I loved to watch movies but hated going to the cinema with all the noise and disruption. It was also where I'd set up my playroom.

Sending the information, and with his follow up agreement to the time and place, I carefully cleaned my Staedtler pen and set my desk to rights. By the time I was showered and changed into a casual pair of Levi's and a lemon polo top, the feeling of excitement had grown to epic proportions. It resulted in me having to tell myself twice to quit getting overexcited and not pin my hopes on something that might turn into only friendship.

Was it a sad state of affairs that I was this excited over a date? *Yeah, it was.*

You're a thirty-six-year old man, get a fucking grip of yourself.

With that ringing through my head, I checked to see if Bailey was in his room to let him know I was off out. Knocking on his door, I waited for several moments. I strained to hear before I walked up to the next level. Bailey was sitting on the two-seater sofa next to the window with a book open in his lap, though I got the feeling he wasn't reading by the distant look on his unguarded face.

It wasn't often I managed to catch him unaware. "Oh, there you are, I'm just off out." I waited for him to look up in my direction before giving him a friendly smile.

His gaze moved over me, and for a moment, I thought I saw a flash of jealousy before he masked his thoughts.

"You got a date?" he bit out, sounding angry. His eyes yet again travelled over the length of my body.

The arousal I kept in check around him buzzed with renewed life. I silently cursed. *Going on a date, remember? He isn't interested in you.*

Then why is he acting like a jealous boyfriend?

"Actually, I do," I answered, careful to keep my tone neutral.

A deep furrow appeared between his brows, but he didn't say anything else.

"I'm not sure how long I'll be gone, but I'll keep the noise down when I get back if I'm late."

"Why, you gonna fuck on a first date?"

I'd already turned to go back down the stairs, but I halted at his muttered comment. Had I heard right?

I looked back over my shoulder and found Bailey's head buried in the book he held. His whole posture was stiff and defensive. I took a steadying breath. "Who I choose to fuck and when is none of your business." The deep tone of my voice got an instant reaction. His shoulders sagged and the hand holding the book trembled.

"I'm sorry…Sir," he answered, his voice full of regret.

I clenched my hands at my sides at the urge to reach out and comfort him. "If you were my sub, I'd cane your backside for this behaviour."

This time his whole body trembled, and I forcibly had to make myself go down the stairs. *Date, you're going on a bloody date.*

A curl of dread undermined my earlier excitement. I worked to swallow past the sour taste in my mouth from going on a date instead of making Bailey's arse red for talking shit to me.

CHAPTER SIX

BAILEY

The air remained trapped in my chest as I waited for the sound of the front door closing in the distance. The arousal Jake's threat had caused throbbed painfully as I set down the book I'd been using to hide it. I glanced down at my lap and cursed my own lack of control around the young Dom.

Sometimes I felt he was totally attuned to me and that scared the fuck out of me. None of the older Doms I'd tended to gravitate to had ever got me so worked up so quickly, just with a threat of what they'd do to me. My hand hovered over my lap, the need to touch vying with an integral part of me that wanted to please his Dom.

He's not your Dom.

I hissed out a loud breath, then heard him leave the house. I was up and running towards the metal staircase tucked into the far corner of the long room. My bare feet slapped against the cool metal as I headed up to the roof terrace to get an unfettered view of Jake as he walked off down the road. I didn't allow myself this privilege often, but with the buzz of arousal flowing through me, I couldn't fight myself any longer.

My nose was nearly flush against the tinted glass that would hide me from view if Jake should turn and look back. He didn't, and for a reason I didn't want to think about too hard, I felt a stab of disappointment.

The jeans and polo top he wore this evening had replaced his usual pressed trousers and shirt he tended to favour, regardless of whether he was working or not. I'd known the minute I'd seen him, there was something different about him. There was an air of excitement about him that was unmistakable, and it twisted me into knots. He had a date. For months he'd seemed only focused on work, and a part of me had breathed easier knowing it. Then he'd appeared with a glow of happiness I'd not witnessed before, and I'd been overwhelmed with a green-eyed monster I wasn't used to.

What right did I have to feel jealous? *None!*

The man had made it more than clear that he was interested in talking about Doming for me. At the time, it had seemed inconceivable, given my feelings for Sam, but then Nathan had set me off on a new path that had left me somewhat confused by my own feelings. I'd never have thought about introducing a third into a relationship, yet now it was all I could think about.

I touched the glass as Jake disappeared from sight, my stomach dropping at the lost opportunity. I'd had every intention of talking to him…*I had!* But I was still reeling after following Nathan's advice of reaching out to Sam.

All right, I didn't exactly reach out to him as I wasn't sure of the reception I'd get. Instead, I'd rung the army base to talk to his sergeant on the pretence of finding out more information about a reunion I'd been invited to. We'd chatted a while before I'd mustered the courage to ask about Sam and how he was getting on after his injury.

What I'd not been expecting was to hear that Sam had been medically discharged from the army months ago. His sergeant hadn't given me any details, and I'd been left so speechless by the information that I hadn't had the wherewithal to ask. I'd spent the whole day stewing over the news in between staring at his picture.

I'd typed, deleted, and then typed again numerous messages, none of which I'd sent.

What had happened to him? Was it his leg, or had there been something else wrong with him? Why hadn't he mentioned anything to me?

You rejected him, why would he tell you anything?

I shut my eyes as the image of the last time I'd seen him in the hospital popped into my mind. The waxy complexion and pinched features. I'd assumed they were the after-effects of recovering from a shrapnel wound and surgery. Had I been wrong? What had the poor boy endured on his own?

I was aware of his past, of his lack of family. He'd have had no one to help him get through whatever he was going through. As I stared out at the busy street below, I shivered uncontrollably, the buzz of arousal long gone.

People were dressed for the warm, sunny evening weather but all I felt was cold. A bone-deep cold that didn't seem to want to leave. I laid my head against the glass, staring unseeingly across the skyline. The warmth penetrating the glass did little to help as a sob rose and got stuck in my throat.

When had these feelings of isolation, of loss, become my constant companion? They swelled in my chest, reminding me of all that I'd turned my back on. A sob tore from me and morphed into a wail. Deep, gut-wrenching sobs poured out of me as I fell to my knees and buried my head in my hands.

For the first time in my life, I let it out. I didn't try to control it or put a lid back on my emotions. It was as if a dam had been breached and there was no way of stopping the deluge that poured out. I'd been taught from a young age by my father that emotions showed weakness, so I'd learned to keep them hidden. I'd used a mask to contain who I really was, and it had been my downfall with Sam. He'd not seen past it, as many had not, to what lay beneath.

I rocked back and forth as I balled my hand into a fist and bit down on it, needing the pain to tether me and stop me from flying apart. The sounds of my distress seemed to reverberate off the glass surrounding me. It prevented me from hiding from my anguish. As my chest burned, tears fell unheeded down my face and dripped onto my shorts.

How was it weak to show how you really felt? My father's words rang through my head, taunting me. *"Real men don't show emotion. Emotions are for the weak and Renfrew men are not weak."*

I gave an angry cry at my father's lack of understanding and for how I'd owned it for too many years. I bit harder at my knuckles and my mouth filled with the coppery taste of blood.

Time passed and my nose became stuffy and my eyes ached from the release. When I felt hollowed out, I wiped at my face with the bottom of my T-shirt, ignoring the tear stains covering my shorts, and my bloody fist. I sucked in a deep breath and shakily released it before I found the energy to stand.

My knees rebelled from kneeling for so long and rubbed salt in an already raw wound, pointing out how long it had been since I'd been in a pose of submission. Plagued by weariness, I slowly dragged my feet over the mosaic tiles covering the floor and headed to the cast iron staircase. My hand trailed over the beautiful metalwork, and I sighed for my own lost dreams.

Back in my bedroom, I stripped and went into the bathroom. In the shower, I slowly washed my body, only then noticing the lack of care with my grooming. When I'd had a Dom, I'd always made sure to wax regularly.

As I looked down at the hair on my chest and groin, my hands balled. *Enough. Enough of the pity party! Enough of not figuring your shit out.* "Enough!" I ground out through clenched teeth.

I huffed out a breath in the steamy cubicle and then another before I stepped out of the shower, dripping water everywhere as I went to find my grooming kit.

Show a little pride. Get your act together and go and fight for what you want!

***

That pep talk carried me through the next day when Jake avoided me. It carried me through all of Saturday, right up until I had to think about getting dressed to go out. The second I'd opened the box of stuff I'd gone to retrieve from the storage unit I'd had for the few merger things I'd collected over the years; my old doubts resurfaced.

Could I wear my harness and leather trousers in front of Jake? The man was somewhere in the house, and I wasn't sure if I could skip out without being seen when Nathan came to collect me. There was also no way I could hide what I chose to wear beneath a big overcoat because it was hot as hell outside and would make it obvious I was hiding something.

Stood naked next to the bed, I eyed the outfit I'd laid out. "Just get dressed," I growled at myself, right as there was a tap at my bedroom door. I froze. My mouth dried, even when my cock plumped knowing who was outside the door.

"Bailey, Nathan, and Lenny are here."

There was a pause, and when I didn't answer, the handle twisted and my pulse skyrocketed. My gaze swept the room, and I cursed my own tidiness when all that was in reach to grab and hide my body were the leather trousers on the bed.

As I reached out with trembling fingers, there was a sharp exhale from the now open doorway, drawing my startled gaze. His expression revealed nothing as his gaze travelled the length of my body.

The following moment of tense silence seemed to stretch as I battled with the urge to grab my trousers instead of standing proud and showing off my body. With the grooming I'd done two days earlier, my whole body was smooth, and although I wasn't as toned as I'd been when in the army, I knew at forty-six, I still looked good.

While I dithered, Jake swung around and turned his back on me. My whole body sagged in defeat. Didn't he like what he saw? A tight band around my chest constricted my lungs and the air remained trapped in my chest, refusing to budge.

"I'm sorry, Bailey, for invading your privacy. When you didn't answer I thought you might have been in the bathroom. I was just going to knock on your bathroom door to let you know the guys were here," he explained, his voice emotionless. "I'll advise them you'll be down shortly." With that, the door shut quietly at his back.

I sank on to the bed, frightened I'd fall if I continued to stand on trembling legs. I rubbed at my chest, hoping to ease the tightness as I struggled to breathe past the crushing reality that I'd lost any chance I might have had with Jake.

Did I really think I deserved someone like him? Someone like Sam?

You do, for fuck's sake, you do!

Then why did it feel like I was trying to wade through fast-drying concrete all the damn time to get to where I wanted to be?

CHAPTER SEVEN

SAM

After eyeing the packed room, I called over to Scott who was stood mixing a drink at the other end of the bar. "Did you reserve a booth for me?"

He was the head-waiter, and unlike the other waiters circulating the room and working in the restaurant who wore white shirts with black dicky bows that had flamingos on, Scott wore a black shirt and his dicky bow was white with pink flamingos. His role in the bar was to manage the bookings for booths when the members wanted to eat, but preferred a less formal setting to the restaurant attached to the bar.

Scott often pitched in behind the bar when we were busy. Tonight was no exception. Both Benny and Shaun, who I'd interviewed with Isaac, were working flat out to keep up with the orders the circulating waiters kept bringing us.

"Yep, but you said you wanted it later, right? The couple in booth two knows they have to leave by eight-thirty as I squeezed them in for a meal." He handed over the drink to the pretty guy he was serving, giving him a bright smile as he took the cash before turning to look at me. His smile transformed into a wicked grin. "You got a hot date tonight?"

Saturday nights in the bar had proven to be busy over the last seven weeks since opening night. Nathan had set up different kink-nights to allow those less comfortable being exposed to all kinks to come and meet new people who liked what they were into. Saturday nights had proven exceedingly popular, with Daddy-kink having had the most attendees to date.

I'd discovered that night that both restaurant owners, Carl and Seb, were Daddies, though Carl was a Daddy Dom so Adam, his husband, had explained. Adam's best friend Richie was Seb's boyfriend/boy, and they'd made it their mission when they'd been introduced to me by Scott to befriend me when they heard I was new to the area. Scott also had a Daddy, Luke, who I'd met on the opening night.

Ferron, who I'd become firm friends with, had encouraged me to get to know the guys when he'd come on the Daddy-kink night with Isaac, who it turned out was his Daddy. It was all a bit mind boggling. That being said, for the first time in my life, I had friends who not only enjoyed kink, but it was as vital to their lives as it was to mine.

I'd always been careful about revealing what I was into in the past because of the army. Though it had become more accepting of the LGBT community, puppy play might have been a little too far-left-field for them.

Tonight, Nathan had opted for a free for all evening with a mix of kinks, which is why I'd messaged Jake to invite him along. I glanced away from Scott for a moment and found the couple of men dressed as puppies. How would Jake react to these?

I grinned back at Scott, anticipation of what was to come buzzing through me, and gave him a saucy wink. "Maybe."

He laughed and rolled his eyes at me. "Bloody tease." He was interrupted by yet another person coming up to the bar, and I went back to filling the large order of drinks. How had I got so lucky to land this job?

What about meeting Jake? Wasn't that lucky too? Butterflies fluttered in my belly, increasing the buzzing anticipation, and I lowered my hand to rub at it. When I'd reached out to him, I'd not expected such a quick response. Yet the second I'd read his message; I'd found myself going with honesty and it had been scary as fuck. The offer to meet had thrown me into a tizzy and I'd got carried away in the moment. I'd not admit how I'd spent the remaining time as I got ready to go out, stressing big time.

Bailey's rejection had left me with major doubts about being able to put myself out there again. Add in my leg, and those doubts turned into fucking major cling-ons that refused to let go.

I wasn't sure what it was about Jake, but the moment I'd laid eyes on his smiling face my anxiety levels had decreased and the knots in my stomach had relaxed enough for me to enjoy the evening. Not sure what to expect, because all I'd had was a picture of a drool worthy backside in leather chaps, I'd been more than a little enthusiastic that the rest of him had matched his arse. He was as fit as fuck, pleasing to the eye, and older than me.

Those were all great, but he'd also turned out to be a decent guy. There had been none of those horrible awkward moments of silence between us as we'd eaten. I wasn't sure if that was because Jake was such a fascinating person or because he'd seemed genuinely interested in getting to know me.

Although Jake was only six years older than me, he carried an air of authority about him that made him appear much older, which was sexy as all hell. I'd discovered as a teenager I preferred to date older men, normally with a bigger age gap than six years. Boys around the same age as me all seemed immature, and somehow, even when I'd matured, I'd remained drawn to older men.

An image of Bailey sprang into my mind and I forcibly shoved it aside. *Not the time nor place. Come on, you invited a man to meet you at work!*

I finished filling the order and placed it on the already loaded tray and beckoned one of the passing waiters, Troy. The cute blond gave me a beaming smile. "Can you take this to booth eleven, please?"

"Yeah, sure. It's rammed tonight and it's still early." Troy, a skinny guy who looked like he needed a good feed, hefted up the tray like he was in a weight training competition and sauntered off, his tiny hips swaying hypnotically.

I chuckled as he worked his way to the booth. The man was a flirt and loved attention, but he was friendly and good-natured and got on with everyone.

When my leg started to throb, letting me know I'd been standing for too long, I grabbed my perching stool. It sat tucked in a cubby hole that Boyd, the contractor, had made special to house it.

A flare of heat spread in my chest at Nathan's considerate nature. He'd never once mentioned my disability or made me feel less as he'd quietly gone about making sure the bar area was suitable for me. It was Scott who'd let slip that Nathan had got Boyd to adapt some of the plans for behind the bar to make it easier for me. The lack of fuss he'd made allowed me to swallow my pride and thank him, though it had taken me a couple of weeks to muster the nerve to mention it.

I searched the room for the man in question. He'd said he was coming with his sub, Lenny. There was no sign of them. Had I got it wrong? Nathan often popped in, but he'd not spent a night in the bar as yet, and I chewed on my lower lip. Was he coming tonight to check up on me? Isaac had shown me the ropes, and so far, I'd been able to keep on top of everything. The only issue I'd had was with the dreaded Excel spreadsheets. Thankfully, Isaac had given me a couple of templates he'd created, so I'd been able to figure out what to do. As far as I could see, I'd not shown any cause for Nathan to be concerned. Then why had he decided to spend the night here?

With no obvious answer, I shrugged off the niggle of worry he was possibly checking up on me and went back to filling the drink orders.

After placing the last drink on the bar and motioning to a different waiter, Mal, I reached for the bulldog clip that held the orders. About to take the next one, I caught movement out of the corner of my eye and my hand stilled. The noise in the busy bar seemed to fade into the background as a loud buzzing started in my ears.

As if in slow motion, my head twisted towards the group of four men walking up to the bar. *No way! No fucking way! It can't be!*

I swallowed hard. Had he come looking for me?

I blinked owlishly, hoping my imagination was playing tricks on me. But no, there stood Bailey right next to...Jake!

Sweet fuck, look at the pair of them!

Sweat slicked my palms as my gaze travelled hungrily over Jake and Bailey, only then noticing what Bailey wore. My eyes widened while my heart decided to be a jockey at the Grand National and took off so fast I couldn't take a decent breath.

Soft-looking, brown leather trousers hugged his muscular legs. There was a delicate leather harness in the same colour wrapped around his massive shoulders and broad chest. Although the outfit screamed Dom, there was something about his posture that said something completely different...*he's submissive*. Fuck, how had I never noticed this? Fingernails dug into my palms and the bite of pain told me this was real. I wasn't going to wake up and find myself in my flat, dreaming.

A thought popped into my head, and pain lanced my already battered heart. Was this why he'd rejected me? A ball of tears lodged in my throat as my gaze met his dark grey, troubled eyes and stunned expression. The tiny flicker of hope that he'd come to find me was smothered.

He rejected you, remember?

Like I need reminding of that.

Chapter Eight

Jake

It took only two seconds for me to realise that something was terribly wrong when Sam, after his initial appreciative glance, didn't pay any attention to me. No, the second his gaze latched onto Bailey, he'd stood transfixed. There were so many emotions flitting over his face; hunger, hope, happiness, and something that pinched at my heart...love. It was unmistakable and it stamped on the seed of expectation I'd felt after our date.

A replay of the evening ran through my mind.

I gave myself a stern talking-to as I walked to Black & Blue Steakhouse at Notting Hill Gate.

Bailey has shown you multiple times he's not interested in what you have to offer.

Then why does he react so beautifully to any show of my dominance?

My cock plumped, not getting on board that this was not the time or the place. I quickened my pace, regardless of the fact that the evening was still warm enough to make me sweat. With the bar in sight, I slowed, not wanting to arrive a sweaty mess if my date was there before me.

The Black & Blue Steakhouse was a place I'd been to several times before and the food never disappointed. When I'd rung up to book, I'd managed to snag a booth, hoping it would give us a little more privacy for me to get to know Sam.

We'd exchanged first names, and when I actively stopped thinking about Bailey, my excitement for the evening returned. I stepped out of the muggy heat into the air-conditioned steakhouse and breathed a sigh of relief at the brush of cooling air against my bare arms.

The place was busy, and I could barely hear the soft music playing in the background over the sound of voices. I waited to be seated. A girl who looked about college-age, dressed in a simple white T-shirt and fitted black trousers, led me to a booth tucked in the corner.

As I sat, I checked my Rolex and ordered a craft beer when the waitress handed me a menu. When she returned a few minutes later, I took the beer, thanking her absently as I watched the door. My tendency to be early for everything left me drumming my fingers on the table as I sipped at my pint. By the time a sole guy walked through the door, I had a nice buzz going on, having not eaten anything all day.

As his gaze swept the room, my stomach lurched when the same eyes from Sam's profile pic met mine. Those same eyes captured my attention, held mine, and for a second, everyone else disappeared. I lifted my hand, and it didn't hurt my ego one bit when his gaze showed real appreciation as I stood.

Low in my belly, I felt a tug of arousal when his eyelashes lowered in a show of submissive behaviour. I gave him a lazy smile as I returned the appraisal. His shaggy, blond-brown hair was layered about his pretty face. He was lean, with slim hips, but his upper torso hinted that his body might be ripped under the V-neck, tight, black T-shirt he wore tucked into low slung jeans. He wore a black leather choker and had several leather bracelets around his left wrist that gave him a sexy vibe.

Sam hesitated for a moment, his smile dimming, and at first, I wasn't sure why, but then he scanned the floor before walking towards me. His hips rolled in a slightly awkward way.

His gaze dropped as he approached, and I had to resist reaching out to reassure him. Instead, I held my hand out. "Hey, I'm Jake, you must be Sam, right?" As I spoke, I took his hand. The rough skin on his palms rubbed against my soft flesh and a shiver raced down my spine.

"Hi"—he glanced about— "nice place. I've not been in London that long, so I'm still figuring out where the decent places to go are." He sounded nervous as he spoke while remaining standing.

I indicated to the seat next to me in the booth, keeping hold of his warm hand, liking the feel of it in mine. "Why don't you sit, and I'll order you a drink. I can recommend the craft beer they have on tap."

He met my suggestion with a smile, seeming to relax as the tension released from his shoulders. I found myself inundated with questions the *moment he sat down, and I released his hand, somewhat reluctantly.*

As the evening had progressed and I'd listened to Sam talk about what had happened to him, I'd found the initial tug of arousal deepen to attraction. I blinked the Flamingo Bar back into focus when the sounds of music and laughter pulled me from my thoughts.

As I looked at Sam now, who remained in the same spot staring at Bailey, I was reminded of that fact.

Sam was so much more than a pretty face. There was something powerful about how he'd picked himself up after a life-changing event and decided not to have a pity party but move on with his life. A life he might have been open about when it came to his injury, but he'd clearly held back the part where he was in love with someone else.

Why did he sign up for an app when he had feelings for someone else? The evening we'd spent together and the offer yesterday to meet here tonight, said Sam was interested in more. So, what was I missing here?

I rubbed at my jaw as my mind mentally started to erect, much as I would a building, an image as I eyed the men around me. Nathan, Sam, and Bailey had all been in the army. Bailey had been Nathan's sergeant, but had he also been Sam's? With my instincts humming, I'd guess I was spot on the money with that. The what's and the why's, that was more difficult to fathom.

Could this be why Bailey carried a bucket-load of sadness about with him? Was he in love with Sam? My eyes narrowed on both men, who it seemed couldn't take their eyes off each other. It appeared they'd forgotten where they were and that there were other people in the noisy bar.

I hissed out a breath when my stomach nosedived to the floor. Resigned to letting any ideas of a relationship with Sam go, I glanced at Nathan.

My heartrate increased at the calculating expression he wore that probably revealed far more than I suspected he knew. Had this been a set-up so that Bailey and Sam could meet?

When Nathan had arrived to collect Bailey earlier this evening, I'd been surprised. *But not as stunned as you were to find a naked Bailey.*

I shut the thought down before I brought up the image of Bailey's drool-worthy body. It had been hard to keep a thought in my head, when he'd come into the living room dressed in leather trousers and a jacket to hide his upper body, with the lingering image of all that smooth, tanned skin.

Keep your head in the game. These men are not for you! The second the voice pointed out the obvious, Sam seemed to regain his senses. He glanced at me with a look of longing that stole my breath before he glanced back at Bailey, who was now staring at the floor.

"It seems the evening has got off to a rather awkward start," I pointed out, going with honesty.

When Lenny nudged at Nathan's arm, wearing a look of 'I told you so', I gave a humourless chuckle. "Are you trying to play matchmaker again?" I asked in a low tone, so my voice didn't carry to the others. Bailey remained silent.

In the past, Nathan had played matchmaker with Carl and Adam. He'd invited Adam to The Playroom unbeknownst to Carl. It had all kicked off when Carl came to the club and found another Dom, Gabriel, trying to stake a claim with Adam.

A red hue slashed across Nathan's cheekbones and he coughed as if he'd got something stuck in his throat. "I...well...it's..."

He trailed off as Bailey finally lifted his head and looked at Nathan with confusion. "Is this why you insisted I come here tonight, because of"—his gaze moved to Sam, who'd finally moved to pour drinks, his head hung down and his gaze on what he was doing—"Sam." He released a shuddery breath, his gaze returning to Nathan.

"Why? Why didn't you say anything?" His face showed betrayal before he swung around and marched off.

"I told you this was a bad idea! Interfering in people's love lives is wrong," Lenny stated in a strident tone that caught several people's attention.

Nathan rubbed at his face before he gave Lenny an apologetic smile. "Yes, it would seem so. But you, my sweet little sub, need to remember that being cheeky to your Dom will only land you in hot water."

Lenny didn't look in the least bit contrite. If anything, he looked a little more defiant as he poked out his chin. "I'm only pointing out what I said to you when you told me about this hare-brained idea of yours." A scowl appeared before he looked at me, then that disappeared to be replaced by a sympathetic smile.

Why was he looking at me like that?

"It's a good thing that Jake is so understanding about your idea of him being their third, otherwise you might have found yourself in—"

I blinked twice, my gaze shifting to Nathan. "What the fuck! What is Lenny talking about?" I demanded in an angry tone. My jaw ached with the control it took not to show the full extent of the anger bubbling inside me like a boiling kettle.

Nathan lifted his arms in a placating manner while he glared at Lenny. "I think we maybe need to take this to my office so I can explain."

Lenny crossed his arms over the see-through mesh top he wore and gave Nathan a stubborn look. "You go to the office. I'm going to get a drink...Sir."

When he answered in such a petulant tone, I folded my lips together to stop them twitching at the show of disobedience, even though I was still furious with Nathan.

Lenny had matured into a wilful sub and he kept Nathan on his toes. Nathan cupped his cheek gently, but his eyes darkened. "We'll talk about this behaviour later. Go and have a drink but stay at the bar until I come back." It was a clear demand.

Lenny lowered his eyes, offering his submission, then spoilt it with cheekiness. "All right, if you insist, Sirrrrr."

This time I couldn't stop the chuckle as Nathan stalked off, shaking his head muttering, "How did I end up falling for a bloody cheeky sub?"

I didn't answer him as I followed, my mind going back over what Lenny had revealed.

The second I shut the door to Nathan's office, I glared at him and demanded, "Care to explain what the hell Lenny was talking about out there?"

Nathan looked resigned as he took a seat in front of his desk and pointed to the chair next to it.

I sat and clenched my hands together in my lap, albeit reluctantly.

"On Thursday, I insisted Bailey come and see me. Months he's been avoiding me, and I wanted answers. After he confessed to being in love with a man who'd been under his command, I put two and two together. Then Bailey showed me a picture and confirmed my suspicions. Up until that point, I'd had no idea what was going on with him."

He stopped speaking and rubbed a hand over his mouth, his gaze turning speculative. For some reason, I found it difficult to take an even breath.

"What I'm about to say I want to remain in the strictest confidence—"

"Bailey's in love with Sam. And I'd go so far as to say that the feeling is mutual after Sam's reaction to seeing Bailey. He was easy to read," I stated gruffly, stopping Nathan in his tracks.

"You're right, but you're missing a part of the puzzle."

I held up my hand, stopping Nathan from saying anything else. "No, don't tell me anything. It's none of my business." Saying it left a hollow feeling inside me, but it was the right thing to do.

"You couldn't be more wrong. If I'm not mistaken, you're interested in both men and that's perfect for what they both need."

What Lenny had mentioned in the bar now started to make sense. My mouth opened, and instead of telling Nathan to take a long hike off a short pier, I found myself asking, with a flicker of renewed hope, "What do they need?"

CHAPTER NINE

SAM

I rolled over onto my stomach and thumped at the pillow under my head, shifting my right leg onto the pillow I used to cushion my stump. A sharp breath hissed out through my clenched teeth. The pain in my right lower leg, real or imaginary, was kicking my arse tonight.

And I blamed Bailey.

Whenever I got tense and couldn't relax, my right leg paid the price. The physio had explained about muscle memory. Right now, my bloody muscles were recalling how my head hadn't listened to my body. The devastation at seeing Bailey yet again turn his back on me had left me tense and edgy. So, I'd done what my old self could easily cope with and worked off my frustration. Only thing was, this new me wasn't as keen on this method at all.

I'd been home three hours, and even the hot and cold packs I'd applied to my leg and the extra strength painkillers I'd taken weren't helping the raw ache inside my non-existent limb.

Rolling onto my back, I stared up into the darkness. A tear slid down the side of my face and into my hair, then another and another until my hair was drenched. It was useless to try and hold in the feelings. I'd learned the hard way that they'd only knock me on my arse later, only it might not be in private.

Jake's face swam before my watery eyes and more tears coursed down my cheeks. The ramifications of not owning my shit were all too clear to see when I'd had the courage to look at Jake. With Bailey no longer the focus of my attention, I'd seen the regret in Jake's eyes, which he didn't try to conceal. That rare honesty left me yearning to go and comfort him.

The bit that had weirded me out after I'd had time to think about it was that the attraction I felt for him hadn't been in anyway diminished when Bailey had stood next to him. If anything, the sight of them together, dressed in leather, left me aroused to the point of pain, especially when I envisioned myself sandwiched between them.

Jake was astute and a Dom, trained to read people, but had he been able to read what I wanted? Would it put him off if I were honest with him? All I had were questions with no real answers as I brought up my hand to swipe at my leaking eyes, sniffing loudly.

When Jake had left with Nathan, Lenny had come to sit at the bar. He'd appeared a little nervous as he'd avoided my gaze and spent most of his time eyeing the door, waiting for Nathan to reappear as he'd sipped at the virgin cocktail I'd made him.

Only on their return did Lenny offer me an encouraging smile I didn't understand before

Nathan had whisked him off. It left Jake alone at the bar with an unreadable expression.

I lifted my head, grabbing the pillow from beneath and plonking it over my face as the conversation we'd had before he'd left ran through my head.

"A minute of your time please, Sam," Jake asked in a tone that sent shivers down my spine.

I'd been counting the seconds off in my head since he'd reappeared, knowing without a shadow of doubt he'd confront me after what had happened. I walked to the end of the bar, stopping next to Scott. "Can you man the bar for a minute or two?"

Scott took one look at my face and his brow furrowed. His gaze moved to Jake, who had walked to the opening at the end of the bar. "Is everything okay?" His voice was a low whisper.

"Not really, but I can't explain right now."

His hand touched my arm. "I'm here anytime you need a shoulder to cry on. I swear I'm good at keeping secrets." He squeezed my arm a little tighter before his hand dropped away.

I nodded, finding it too difficult to speak right then. Stealing a quick look at Jake beneath my lashes, I sucked in a steadying breath then walked to where he stood. I pointed to the door that led into the stockroom. "It might be best to go in there so we can have some privacy." I didn't tag on so that he could dump me after only one date.

The door closed silently at my back, and I leant against it to stop anyone from taking us by surprise. I really didn't want anyone witnessing my humiliation as I raised my gaze to meet Jake's.

"You're in love with Bailey."

It wasn't a question, so I didn't answer.

"Do you want to talk to me about it?" His voice was even, but there was a strained look around his eyes.

"There's really not much to say. I love him, he doesn't love me, end of story." I hated the despair I could hear as I voiced that aloud, but I felt I owed it to Jake to be honest.

"I think there's so much more to this story." He held up his hand to stop me from interrupting as my mouth opened. "I get this is neither the time nor the place. And that you might think I'm no longer interested in you." His nostrils flared as he stepped into my personal space, crowding me against the door. The scent of leather and spicy aftershave filled my nose as I inhaled shakily. The black T-shirt he wore in lieu of a leather harness brushed against me and I could feel the heat of his body penetrate through my thin shirt. "But you couldn't be more wrong."

Feeling dizzy, I attempted to suck in a breath and resisted the urge to press against the firm body in front of me and let him hold me. My lashes fluttered down to hide how overwhelmed I felt at his closeness, from his declaration. Did he really want to keep seeing me, knowing I was in love with another man?

"Eyes on me," he growled low in his throat.

A shiver of excitement ran through me as I did as he requested. He held my gaze, his dark eyes glittering with desire that, for the first time in years, gave me hope I could have feelings for someone other than Bailey. His mouth hovered above mine, and for a moment I thought he might kiss me, then he took a step back. I sagged in disappointment, not missing the glint of satisfaction in Jake's eyes. "I want you to think about what you want from me. Once you're sure you know, message me."

I threw the pillow on the floor in frustration and reached over to the bedside table, needing light. What do I really want? *Goddammit, you know what you want!*

I blinked the white spots from my bleary eyes and sat up enough to rest my back against the wooden headboard. My chest billowed as I sucked in several tremulous breaths. Could I be honest about what I wanted and chance yet another rejection?

Eyeing my phone for a second, I reached for it and pulled up Bailey's contact details. Pulling up the message feed, I sighed at how long it had been since we'd shared even a simple "hey, how are you doing" message. I frowned and stared at the screen, hesitating before typing.

Why didn't you tell me you are a sub?

Not giving myself a chance to rethink it, I hit send. My heartrate accelerated when it immediately came up as 'message read'. I held my breath. Would he answer me? Hope sprung to life as the screen showed he was typing a message. *Oh god, please answer me!*

I sat for long minutes, the pain in my right leg pain long forgotten as the hope turned to misery and became my full focus. The lack of message was answer enough. *He doesn't want me.* "He might not want me, *but Jake does.*"

Maybe that could be enough?

***

With little to no sleep on Saturday night and another busy shift at the bar today, I felt drained and glad I had the following day off. I lay on the bed and switched on the TV after a quick shower to rid myself of the smell of stale alcohol. With thoughts about messaging Jake after the continued radio silence from Bailey, I was too wired to sleep.

I'd spent most of the last twenty-four hours thinking about what Jake had said. It turned out what I really wanted was way kinkier than I'd anticipated. I couldn't think past the picture of me tucked between the two men. Wasn't that just my fucking luck? I find someone that's interested in me, and then I want to fuck that up with my kinkiness.

Running my hands through my damp hair, I stared blankly at the TV. Why the fuck did life have to be so damn complicated? *What happened before was so easy? Not!*

Get over yourself and message Jake and be honest. He isn't going to accept anything less than that and you shouldn't either. Remember what you've already faced and overcome.

The empty space at the bottom of the bed was an all too obvious reminder. I glanced at it, then reached for the phone I'd dropped on the bed.

It wasn't like I was hiding anymore; Jake knew everything. *Well, almost.* So what was stopping me from messaging him?

The answer was way too obvious, and I huffed out a frustrated breath. I checked the time on my phone before opening The App. Was it too late to message at midnight?

Playfulpuppy: *I've a day off tomorrow. Do you have any free time?*

As I hit send, I released the breath I hadn't been aware I'd been holding. It gave Jake an out if he'd changed his mind. My fingers tightened around the phone. *Please don't let him change his mind about me.*

My gaze became riveted to the phone when the bubbles appeared, and it showed he was typing. Recalling my huge disappointment from the night before, I shut my eyes to block out the screen. After several long seconds, my hands grew clammy and with my stomach knotting, I pried one eye open to look at the screen.

Opentoeverything: *Perfect, I'll rearrange my appointments for later in the week to clear my day. Bring your puppy gear to this address...*

My eyes blurred and my body sagged against the bed. Bring my puppy gear...holy fuck!

CHAPTER TEN

JAKE

I stared at Bailey's untouched bed for the second day in a row, my temper coming to a boil. Where the fuck was he?

Nathan was adamant he wasn't staying with him, and that he had no clue where the man had gone after he'd left the club on Saturday night. I'd understood that he'd been blindsided by Nathan, and that he'd been brought face to face with something he'd still been struggling with, as far as I could tell, but that was no excuse for disappearing.

Nathan had been apologetic for his part in the fuck-up that had been Saturday night. It was only his insistence that he'd wanted what was best for all three of us that had convinced me to hear him out fully and not kick his arse. Although that might have been a mean feat with him being a fucking demon in the boxing ring. I'd watched him once with Isaac and that was enough for me to keep my threat to myself because I wasn't stupid.

I'd had time to get my head around his suggestion that maybe both men would fulfil the needs I'd struggled with. Individually, neither a sub nor a boy had worked for me, and I found myself warming to the idea of trying something a little different. Only, one of the vital parts of the equation, Bailey, had gone AWOL. Any hope to speak to him before Sam arrived this morning was dead in the water.

I'd messaged Bailey several times to check he was okay, only he'd not read any of my messages. I'd double-checked to make sure I had the right number and had even gone so far as messaging Nathan to check there was nothing wrong with my phone.

There was bugger all wrong with my phone. No, Bailey was playing hide-and-fucking-seek with me. A game, he was going to find, that ended with him tied up and his arse reddened. My fingers twitched in anticipation of using a cane to spank the naughty sub's fucking arse until he remembered to answer his bloody messages.

You're getting ahead of yourself.

That might be so, but I knew what Bailey needed and I was going to give it to him. With that conviction running through me, I stomped out of the empty room and headed downstairs, working at pushing the worry I felt for Bailey aside.

The anger came from a deep-rooted concern I'd developed for the stoic man after months of watching him suffer in silence. A silence I now understood. That, however, wasn't going to spoil the rest of my plans for today or what I planned for Bailey's return.

If he wasn't prepared to face his feelings right then, there was nothing I could do about it. Sam, on the other hand, had reached out, and though I wanted Bailey to be a part of what was going to happen today, I wasn't going to cancel my plans.

That would be too much like a punishment for Sam, and I wanted to reward him for his bravery.

Walking down the two flights of stairs, I went down the hallway and into my playroom. I inhaled the scent of incense and leather as I switched on the lights and glanced about the room. A buzz of expectation ran through me and my hands trembled at thoughts of what was going to happen when Sam stepped into this room.

When I'd designed the house, I'd always known I'd want my own playroom. I'd been a member of a BDSM club since the age of twenty, but I'd always promised myself a room of my own to play in when I built my own home. With that in mind, I'd given what was going to go in this room a hell of a lot more consideration than I had for any other room in the house.

I ran my hand over the built-in floor to ceiling oak cabinet doors that lined two full walls. They housed my extensive array of toys I'd collected over the years. The remaining two walls were a deep blue that my decorator had argued would be too dark with the amount of wood and no window in the room. I'd not bothered to explain my choices. Instead, I'd ignored them and gone ahead with my plans with the knowledge and vision of how it would look when it was finished. I'd not been disappointed, and my decorator had been wrong.

The room was anything but dark with the up-lighters I'd had placed around the top of all the walls. They reflected a pink, dreamy light over the cream ceiling. It gave the room an ethereal feel, offering the intimate atmosphere I wanted for when I played.

I'd not put a bed in this room as it was only fifteen by thirteen feet, and though not small, I'd had to compromise when I'd decided I'd wanted a cinema room on this level too. I refused to think about how that room had seen more action than this one. With my last sub turning out to be more hardwired towards pain than I was comfortable with, we'd parted ways amicably. We were still on speaking terms, but it was a little difficult to watch him at the club with his new Dom. I'd not loved him, but I'd had deep feelings for him which had taken time to fade.

Downloading The App had been about me getting back on the horse and finding out what I wanted. That hadn't worked out quite as I'd expected. Maybe this new turn of events would give me what I'd been searching for?

The message Sam had sent last night opened the door to many new possibilities. Would he be open to listening to me? I'd hardly got a wink of sleep thinking about it all. I'd noticed the couple of men dressed in puppy gear on Saturday, but it was more in passing than paying any real attention with everything else.

As I eyed the gleaming wooden floor. I considered what a puppy might need. The plush, navy, velvet armchair, which was big enough to sit two comfortably, sat a little more in the middle of the room, in front of the St. Andrew's Cross.

Pushing it over the floor, I put it against the bare wall. Then I walked back over to the St. Andrew's Cross, tipping it onto the wheels that allowed me to move it alone. I placed this into the far corner. Next went the navy leather spanking bench until it butted up against the side of the chair, leaving the centre floor free.

I pictured myself sat in the armchair as Sam ran around on his hands and knees, and with it came a flood of arousal. I chuckled at how many times I'd questioned whether I'd enjoy this kind of play. My plumping cock showed just how much it had appreciated the visual.

When the doorbell peeled loudly, seconds later, my cock thickened further. I gave it a painful squeeze to take the edge off my growing arousal before I felt decent enough to go and answer the door.

My hand shook with eagerness as I opened the door and found Sam stood holding a leather hold-all clutched tightly in his hands. His face was a little pale, but his eyes gleamed with a determination that left me a little breathless.

"Hey," Sam said, speaking so quietly I could hardly hear him.

"Hey yourself," I answered, stepping back to let him step in.

When he did without question and lowered his gaze to the floor, releasing a tremulous breath, I understood in that moment what he was offering me. He was about to expose his vulnerability to me, knowing I could possibly reject him. I'd never do that, but he didn't know that. Didn't know that I'd researched what assistance amputees needed so I could be prepared to make this experience as special as possible for him.

My heart swelled, making it impossible to speak or swallow as my emotions ran amok. The Dom in me wouldn't allow the moment to pass without acknowledging what he was offering me so freely, so I reached out a hand to touch his cheek. I swallowed to wet my dry mouth. "Thank you for trusting me."

His eyes gleamed with unshed tears that tugged at my heart, making it impossible to move my gaze from his. He nodded in acknowledgement but remained silent as I stroked his cheek gently. The soft sigh he released was like music to my ears.

There was the blare of a horn, and Sam jerked and looked out the still open door before looking back at me, chuckling. "Maybe we should shut the door. I don't want to give your neighbours a free show." Although it was said in a jokey tone, it was filled with nerves he couldn't hide.

CHAPTER ELEVEN

SAM

I mentally cursed the nerves in my voice as Jake gave me one of his lazy smiles that set my pulse racing. No amount of trying to figure out how I'd feel when I stepped into Jake's home to play for the first time had prepared me for the moment that had passed between us.

There was something different about Jake in that instant that set off a tremor inside me that I'd only ever felt for one other man—Bailey. I'd made a decision not to mention Bailey unless Jake brought up the topic first. The last thing I wanted was for that to come between us with so much uncertainty. Was I headed towards yet another heartbreak? Could I cope if I fell for Jake and he denied me in the same way Bailey had?

A shiver of apprehension ran through me as the lock snicked on the door behind me. As if Jake understood where my head had gone, his hand returned to my cheek.

"Look at me, Pup."

I swallowed a groan at his husky demand and use of the word 'pup'. A pulse of intense arousal headed straight for my cock and my jeans suddenly felt too small. I wanted to obey, god I did, but I was frightened by what I'd reveal. It had been too long since I'd played; since I'd felt the freedom of letting go. For more months than I cared to admit, getting my rocks off had only been about getting rid of some tension, nothing more.

Standing with Jake, his hand touching my face the only physical contact between us and his use of that husky rasp, I worried I was about to come in my pants and embarrass myself.

"I won't ask you again, Pup. Look at me."

His voice got incredibly deep and I shuddered, barely able to stop myself from panting as I did as he bid.

His fingers traced down my cheek, then moved around the collar of my T-shirt before taking a firm hold of the back of my neck. His hot, minty breath touched my incredibly warm face as he stared deep into my eyes, leaving me feeling completely exposed. "There's a good Pup. Do you have a safe word?" The words were barely a whisper as his lips brushed against mine in the softest caress.

How was I supposed to answer him when I wasn't even sure anymore if I had the capacity to do more than melt into a puddle at his feet?

His chuckle tickled my lips deliciously before he moved back and looked at me, his smile now wicked. "Safe word, Pup, what is it?"

"Dreamcatcher," I answered on a breathy moan.

"Nice." His fingers tightened on my neck, but not painfully. "When we enter my playroom, I'll trust you to use it if at any point it gets too much for you."

"Yes..." I trailed off, unsure what to call him. Clearly, he was a Dom, but when I'd played before, it hadn't felt right to use any term that denoted the difference between me and the men I'd played with.

His free hand came up and he touched the bridge of my nose. "What's troubling you, Pup?"

The genuine concern I heard released a little of the tension tying my stomach in knots. "I...what...shit—"

His brows rose. "Take a breath for me. That's it. Is this about what you call me?"

"Yes," I said in a breathless rush.

His eyes crinkled at the edges as he dropped the hand touching my brow. "I prefer Sir in the playroom, but if that's too much then Jake will be fine."

"I can do that...call you Sir...I'd like that." I confessed because the minute I took my clothes off, he'd know how much this was turning me on. We'd done nothing and I was raring to go. At the rate my cock was leaking, I'd need to go commando when I left, my underwear was already soaked.

"If you've no other questions, do you want to go into my playroom to play?" It might have sounded like a causal question, but the tension rolling off him steadied my own nerves. That he wasn't unaffected by what was happening between us allowed me to nod.

"I need to hear you say it Pup," he growled, causing more pre-cum to leak into my pants.

"Yes, yes I do...Sir."

The smile that lit his face at my answer appeared brighter than the sun as he beamed at me. I let myself bask in its warmth before he turned and walked off down the hall.

My heart hammered painfully against my ribs as my leg misbehaved for a second on the slippy tile and I had to right myself. Heat rode up my neck and I shut my eyes, sending a silent prayer I wasn't about to make the biggest fool of myself.

"Sam...you okay?"

Realising I must look like a dork stood with my eyes shut, they fired open and I sucked in a breath, squared my shoulders, and walked to Jake. I let out a relieved breath when I reached him without slipping.

"I'm fine...your floors are a little slippy." I hated how hot my face felt, but I met his gaze head on.

He gave the tile a hard stare, then looked back at me. There was no pity, and I relaxed my shoulders. "I'll look into an anti-slip coating."

Did that mean he wanted me to come back again? It seemed so when he said nothing more and entered the room that thankfully had a wooden floor and none of the shiny grey tiles like the hallway. I glanced about as I stepped into the room. My stomach flipped over at the size of the cupboards and what might be hiding in them as Jake pushed the door to.

His bare feet made no noise as he walked over to the padded velvet chair. "Do you want me to help you get changed?"

The excitement in his voice made it easy to answer with an affirmative. He took the bag from me as I stepped to him, and opened it. His eyes became impossibly dark as his pupils disappeared and his cheekbones got splashes of colour over them.

He clearly liked what was in the bag. I trembled as he reached in to touch some of my prized possessions. He handled them with care as he laid them out on the blue velvet chair we were standing next to. I'd immediately noticed that he'd moved the few bits of furniture from the tell-tale scuff marks on the floor.

Although the room wasn't brightly lit, everything was visible. I took the time to familiarize myself with the space as Jake emptied the bag. I sniffed and scented what smelt like the forest.

The touch to my elbow pulled my attention back to Jake. "I'm going to undress you now. Do you need to sit?"

"It will be easier for me that way." The slight quiver in my voice was better than I'd expected when I thought about him touching my body for the first time.

He moved the contents of the bag into a neat pile, making room for me to perch on the cushion. I sunk into the plush cushion, groaning. "Oh god, I could do with a seat like this."

He grinned at me as he lowered himself to his knees in front of me.

Inhaling sharply, I struggled to keep still as Jake undid the laces of my shoes and then removed them. On our date, I'd not plucked up the nerve to show him my leg. Now I wasn't sure if I regretted that.

His hands made quick work undoing my jeans. His hand brushed against my groin and more heat filled my face. He gave me a saucy wink, drawing my attention to the fact that no matter how worried I was about him seeing me naked, my cock wasn't of the same mind.

"Lift your bottom."

Doing as I was told, I held on to the arms of the chair while he tugged my jeans and underwear down together. My cock bounced and slapped at my stomach. Jake swallowed hard, making his Adam's apple bob furiously as he eyed my cock hungrily. His tongue laved at his lips and I imagined what it would feel like against my flesh.

A bead of pre-cum pearled on the tip of my cock and Jake's jaw bunched as he looked away with what appeared to be great difficulty, making me light up inside.

As he slowly peeled my jeans and underwear down my legs to reveal my prosthetic limb, he lent forward and laid a kiss on my exposed thigh. My leg jerked as my stomach fluttered with nerves. His gaze met mine and all I saw was desire.

"Is it okay for me to remove the prosthetic?" His voice was thick with emotion and it tugged at my heart.

I sucked in a shaky breath. *You can do this!* "Yes."

With a little guidance he gently removed the limb and the coverings on my stump. Again, he laid a gentle kiss against the puckered, scared skin. The fluttering inside me increased as I trembled at the adoring look on his face.

By the time I was fully naked, and he'd carefully placed my prosthetic limb to one side, any fear Jake would reject me the minute he saw my leg was lost under a barrage of desire he didn't mask. His face was flushed, his eyes glittered, and the bulge in the front of his shorts more than showed he wasn't in the least bit put off by the sight of me.

"Do I need to put the covering back over the stump?" he asked gently.

"It'll be more comfortable for me with the knee protector if you put one back on."

His fingers gently traced the soft covering as he slipped it back in place. I'd used two coverings to cushion my stump. His eyes showed interest as he reached out to pick up one of my knee protectors. He didn't hesitate to slide it over my stump while holding the edge of the material to stop it rucking up.

I jerked again and he immediately stopped. His gaze moved swiftly to my face. "Do you need to safe word?"

I had to take a breath and think about my answer. The feel of him touching my stump was…different to the kisses. When others had touched me, it had been the nurses and doctors. Their touches had been detached almost. Jake's was anything but impersonal.

I eyed my lap and my still-aroused cock. My thinking head wasn't nearly as quick at making up its mind as my other head, apparently. "I'm…okay…I think. I don't feel the need to safe word."

The approval I saw in his eyes did silly things to my stomach, so I kept my focus on his hands.

CHAPTER TWELVE

JAKE

None of the many scenes I'd done with subs in the past had prepared me for this level of connection so early on in a new relationship. I wanted to believe it was just because this was different, something I'd never done before, but I'd only be fooling myself.

What would it be like if Bailey were here too, watching while strapped to my cross, gagged, plugged, his cock and balls tied up? My hands shook at the wave of dizziness that accompanied the flood of arousal heating my groin. With Jake not mentioning Bailey, I'd left the elephant in the room well alone. We'd need to talk about it, but this appeared not to be the time.

One brick at a time. Remember, nothing that is worth building can be rushed.

A shard of disappointment pierced my bubble of excitement, and I took two deep breaths before I reached for the second knee protector.

Keeping my thoughts in check while I finished making sure his knees were protected, I eyed the gloves, mask, and plaited leather tail that had a small plug at the end. The bottle of lube I'd found in the bag made me smile.

Sam's arousal didn't flag as I moved to stand once I'd put the gloves on his hands. I picked up the beautiful half mask and scented the leather. "It's beautiful, is it hand crafted?"

"Yes...Sir. I had it made to fit my face. I've had all the pieces made over the years as I could afford them."

His voice shook, but he held my gaze as I stepped closer to place the mask over his face. Being careful not to pull his hair, I brushed his fringe out of the way as I moved it into position. His deep-blue eyes staring out at me through the mask left me with butterflies in my gut. I brushed my fingertips over the leather, and he groaned as if he could feel my touch through the mask. His eyelashes lowered and he dipped his head, pushing his head into my hand much as a pup would seek his master's touch.

Holy fuck!

Gently, I stroked over his head, letting him show me what he liked. Long minutes passed as I stood gently running my hands over his head and down the back of his neck and back. He made these lovely little whiney noises in the back of his throat.

His body relaxed fully but his cock remained hard, standing proud from his hairless groin. I petted him for several more minutes before I got back down on my knees in front of him. His head lolled to one side as he eyed me.

"Pup, do you need help to get down onto the floor so I can insert your tail?"

He shuddered and shook his head. About to ask him to use his voice, I realised that would take away from the mood we'd created. So instead, I shifted to the side to give him room and indicated at the floor beside me. "Come on then, Pup, get down."

He made a snuffling noise and moved effortlessly onto all fours. Had he practiced that move? I gave him a smile of approval and rubbed my hand along the length of his golden skinned body to his pale arse.

Tail in hand, I found the lube and slicked up the small plug. It curved in a way that meant it would stimulate him as he moved about.

Sam's body vibrated as he eyed me and the tail. "Turn round, Pup."

He did as requested and presented his arse to me, wiggling it. I chuckled at the playful act. Using the remaining slick on my hand, I slid a finger down the crease of his pert backside. His parted thighs quivered and his arse clenched as I brushed his sensitive hole, letting him get used to the feel of me.

He whined low and long and pushed his arse back into my finger as I pressed against the warm flesh. When he pushed back a second time, I slipped my finger past the tight ring of muscle. He squeezed my digit and rocked as if trying to get me to go deeper. I eased in until my knuckle bumped his arse cheek. I held still as he moaned and rolled his hips as if he were rutting against something. "You like that, Pup? You like your master touching you?"

His whine became high-pitched and his pelvis rocked faster. I laughed as I let him have his fun for a moment before slipping my finger free of his arse. His body swayed before his backside was pushed closer to my face. I slapped his arse cheek, stopping the movement. He panted and his head turned in my direction, his eyes betraying his need.

I gave his other cheek a stinging blow and he rose to meet it, his gaze never leaving mine. A heady surge of need I always got from being with a sub pulsed through me as I lifted the tail and placed it against his slick hole. He quivered but didn't move as I slid the plug into his body.

Heavy-lidded eyes stared at me with desire as I moved the plug in and out of his arse several times before I left it inside him and trailed my fingers down the leather plait. He moaned in delight and his arms shook. He panted while I stroked his rosy, flushed skin, finding enjoyment from his pleasure.

"Pup, you look so beautiful. My cock is so hard right now, all because of you," I rasped through a tight throat.

His low growl made it harder than I liked to stop touching him, but this wasn't about what I wanted right now, it was about what Sam needed. Reluctantly, I stood and walked to the chair, lifting the final thing I'd found in the bag. A small red ball that he'd be able to easily pick up in his mouth.

The second I held the ball up, his face got a silly grin on it that melted my heart. He looked so damn adorable and I found myself responding with a big smile. I threw the ball. "Fetch Pup."

He was off before I'd even finished the command. I laughed as he moved, more gracefully than I'd expected, across the wooden floor. He used his knees and his left foot like an oar to steer him in the direction he wanted to go. He came back with the ball clenched between his teeth, then dropped it at my feet. His face lit with expectation as I bent, picked up the slightly damp ball, and rubbed the top of his head. I feigned throwing it left then threw it the other way, making him have to twist, but he didn't seem in the least bit phased as he raced after the ball.

His exuberance was contagious, I continued to laugh at his antics. I stroked him, rewarding him every time he brought me back the ball. Each time, he'd mewl a little louder. The floor was streaked with drips of pre-cum, his cock flushed with arousal and pointed down at the floor while he moved.

He made an intoxicating sight. The scent of leather and his musk combined to add to my own desire. It got more difficult as it became apparent Sam was getting closer to losing all his inhibitions and coming.

Distracted, I glanced at the partially open door. Had I heard a noise? I tilted my head, straining to hear. Fuck, had Bailey returned? My heart slammed against my ribs as Sam dropped the ball at my feet, his eyes giddy with excitement.

Another noise came from the hall, only this time, Sam heard it to. His eyes widened and all the joy fled from his expression.

Shit, shit, shit!

CHAPTER THIRTEEN

BAILEY

Too distraught to go back to Jake's, and desperate enough not to worry about imposing on Ferron, I'd rung him from outside the club on Saturday night. He'd answered and immediately offered me a bed for the night.

I'd gone into The Playroom, and Isaac had given me a spare key to his home and organised for an Uber to take me there. He'd not asked any questions, though they'd been written on his face.

I'd escaped with Ferron's reassurance that they wouldn't let on they'd seen me. That had been two days ago, and I was still hiding out in their spare room, having borrowed some of Isaac's clothes.

The messages from Nathan and Jake remained unopened, but the message I'd received from Sam in the early hours of Sunday morning had been too hard to resist. The accusation was now burned into my memory banks, never to be erased again.

Why didn't you tell me you are a sub?

As always, Sam didn't hide from the hard questions, from demanding answers no matter how painful they might be for both of us.

How can it be hard for you? You've not bothered to answer him. You've done nothing but avoid facing him and the truth. What happened to your little speech no more than four days ago?

"Oh, fuck off," I grumbled to the voice in my head.

"Well that's not very nice, now is it?" Ferron answered as he sailed into the bedroom with a determined look on his face.

Here was another man that was battling his demons and trying to make a better life for himself. You take a good look at him. Shame heated my cheeks as I stared at him. "I was talking to myself," I mumbled.

"I know that. I do it a lot, especially when I'm trying to get Devon out of my head." His face became pinched with sorrow.

I reached out and touched his arm, careful not to spook him when he sat on the bed next to me. "I'm sorry for reminding you of Devon."

He patted my hand. "Oh, you don't have to apologise for that. That fucker is to blame for that and no one else. But with Mark's help and Isaac's love, his voice isn't as strong anymore." He licked his lips, took a deep breath, then said in a rush, "Talking helped me to sort out my head. Maybe it could help you too? I'll listen if you like."

A sob choked me, and I swallowed hard. *Come on, be brave.*

I repeated pretty much what I'd told Nathan, only this time it was a little easier to say it aloud. To admit what I'd done to both of us. "I knew I'd never be able to give him what he needed, so I'd resigned myself to living a life without him. Then

Nathan puts an idea in my head right before Sam shows up in the one place I wasn't expecting to see him, The Flamingo Bar." My voice cracked and Ferron edged a little closer.

He took the hand I'd placed on his arm and intertwined our fingers, squeezing them in encouragement. "Is it Sam?" he asked hesitantly.

"Yes, yes, it is." Agony I'd lived with since that fateful night gripped my heart, exposing me to what I'd denied us both...an opportunity to try. "I was a coward because I put my own needs first and because of that, I lost a precious gift I should have treasured."

His fingers tightened around mine. "How do you know it's lost when you haven't spoken to him? Life has taught me a valuable lesson. Hiding behind your fear doesn't solve anything."

He laid his head on my shoulder and gave a happy sigh. "It can be painful to poke at your fear, but once you do, you can learn to see that it's you that has control, not it. You need to think about the rewards. Focus on what you want, not on what you don't. I swear it will make all the difference."

The utter conviction in his voice helped me face what had been on my mind since I'd seen Sam and the emotions he'd not hidden from me. "Can I ask you a question?" His head nodded on my shoulder.

"Do you think me suggesting bringing in a third person, a Dom, would be the right thing to do?" I held my breath as Ferron's head lifted and I chanced a look at his face.

His brow furrowed and he got a contemplative look in his eye. Several seconds passed before he spoke. "I'm not sure what Sam is into, but he's a submissive at heart, so I'd say if he loves you then he'd be open to the suggestion." His eyes twinkled. "Personally, I think it's hot, but don't tell Isaac I said that," he whispered.

I chuckled at his cheeky wink and quick look at the open door. "I won't say anything."

He grinned at me. "Do you have someone in mind for a third?" His brows wiggled up and down.

My chuckles turned into full blown laughter as I choked out, "I might."

"It's Jake, isn't it? He's a total hottie. That confident, sexy businessman that hides a naughty side, is—"

"Naughty side is…what?" came Isaac's none-too-happy voice from the doorway.

I glanced at Isaac and relaxed at the humour dancing in his eyes as Ferron lifted his head off my shoulder.

"Is what I love about my Daddy," he finished, getting up off the bed and sauntering to Isaac with a confidence that hadn't been visible when I'd first met him at Adam's stag party.

"Is that right?" Isaac's mouth spread into a wide grin before he bent to kiss the tip of Ferron's nose. "Then maybe you need to remind me—"

"Daddy, we've a guest," Ferron's face was fire-engine-red as he glowered at Isaac.

"Actually, I'm going to head back to Jake's and…have a chat with him," I finished lamely.

Ferron gave me a look of approval, whereas Isaac looked more than a little relieved.

Quickly making my exit when the Uber arrived to take me to Jake's, I thanked them both again before hopping into the car.

I gave myself yet another pep talk about manning up and owning my feelings. With all the past conditioning I'd had, it was hard to not slip back into old habits and worry about revealing my true feelings.

My hands clenched in my lap as the driver weaved through the busy Monday traffic. Nathan and Ferron had battled their demons and won, so why couldn't I?

The years of giving in, of being conditioned to do what others want, were gone.

Really?

I closed my eyes, hoping to shut out the voice. Wasn't I entitled to claim the life I wanted? Ferron's word floated through my mind. *Focus on what you want, not what you don't want.* Did that include Jake? There was no denying that I felt something for the Dom, but was it only arousal? What if he wasn't interested in Sam? Where would that leave me, leave Sam? Surely, I'd be back to square one, unable to give Sam what he needed.

Stop borrowing trouble. Focus on what you want, remember.

Sam. I wanted Sam. And...Jake? *Maybe.*

It continued to circle around my head as the car stopped outside Jake's house. Exiting the car after thanking the driver, I stood on the curb, digging my hand in shorts I'd borrowed off Isaac to pull out my house keys.

The heat of the sun pressed against my skull as I stood for long minutes, working up the courage to go inside and seek out Jake. "Focus on what you want," I muttered under my breath, trying to give myself some Dutch-courage before walking up the stone path.

You've faced much worse situations than this.

Yeah, but they never involved my heart before.

Yeah, facing death was so much easier.

I rolled my eyes at the voice arguing back and forth and blew out a frustrated breath as I opened the front door. I was met with silence as I slipped off my boots and walked over the grey marble tiles to the stairs that led up to the bedrooms.

Hand on the railing, I stilled at a muffled laugh coming from the other end of the hallway. I'd not explored this part of the house because Jake spent quite a bit of time working in his office, which was housed on this floor. When he'd shown me through the house, I'd questioned why he had his office on the ground floor. He'd laughed, saying he'd get nothing done for looking out the window at all the wonderful architecture. I'd not understood that until he'd started to point out and talk about some of the buildings you could see from his third-floor windows.

It was one of the few times I'd found myself relaxing around him. His passion for his work was like the first rain after a long drought. It soaked past the dry cracks of what had been my life and watered the seeds of my own hidden dreams to be a full-time sub.

There was another muffled laugh, so full of joy that I found the pull to go and investigate, irresistible. My feet padded silently over the cool tiles as I walked to the end of the hallway.

You shouldn't spy on Jake!

It was too late to listen to reason when I saw the door, where I thought the laughter was coming from, was partially open. There was enough of a crack to allow me to squint and peer through.

My heart twisted in my chest and made it impossible to breathe. My feet appeared glued to the floor as if I'd been clamped for illegal parking. In a way I had, only I was watching something I clearly wasn't meant to see.

A painful throbbing started in my neck and worked its way up into my skull, but I couldn't seem to take my eyes off the sight before me. A surge of arousal flared through me and I clung to the doorframe, then the air hissed out past my lips as Jake moved to the left to fully reveal the man dressed as a puppy. The man wore a black leather mask that covered the top half of his face and his hair. He wore black gloves and knee pads. But it was the glimpse of something moving at his rear and his hard, leaking cock that drew my gaze.

Then the puppy spun around to chase whatever Jake had tossed out of view. It was then I caught sight of his legs and my gut twisted into painful knots. I dry-heaved and was alerted to the fact I'd not taken a breath by the fire in my chest. Even with all that, my mind was crystal clear as the puppy spun back around, his aroused cock bouncing as it dripped on the floor, showing how excited he was. The puppy's head lifted, and eyes that I'd dreamed about stared up at Jake with the same adoration that had once been aimed at me, and they ripped my world apart. I staggered, my back thudding against the wall.

CHAPTER FOURTEEN

SAM

I was alerted to the fact something was wrong by Jake's sudden stillness. It was the noise coming from the hallway that gave me cause for concern. I stared between the partly open door and Jake. Had someone been watching us? Had Jake set me up? I discarded the thought the moment it registered. He looked just as shocked as me.

He, however, was quicker to react as he charged for the door and threw it open. My mouth opened but no words came out. *Bailey! Bailey was here? How? Why? Oh Christ!*

The thoughts whirled around my head as Bailey looked between me and Jake, his expression revealing too many emotions to fathom them all. But one was clear, betrayal.

It cut at my heart, until I recalled how he'd rejected me. I hardened my heart, or at least tried to. I ripped off my mask and dropped it on the floor, followed quickly by my tail, feeling far too vulnerable and exposed to leave them in place.

"Bailey, where the fuck have you been for the past two days?" Jake demanded, stunning me into immobility.

Why is he asking where Bailey has been?

"What the fuck is going on here?" I gritted out, my

jaw aching as my teeth ground together. With nothing making sense, my own anger started to simmer.

Bailey continued to lean against the wall as if his legs couldn't hold him, his eyes sweeping over my naked body and stopping on my flagging arousal. *Fucking hell!*

How had I gone from having fun, to this hell? Truly, what the fuck! As I went to crawl to my clothes, Jake stopped me with his next words.

"Pup, wait." His gaze held mine for a moment, and I struggled to read the meaning in his eyes before his head moved and stared at Bailey. "Bailey, come in here, now."

Bailey's head hung down, but not before I noticed the flare of arousal in his dark eyes from the Dom's demand. He moved, albeit reluctantly, into the room, not making eye contact with either of us.

Jake seemed to take a moment as he licked his lips, then he met my gaze and all I could see was a hunger that got my flagging cock to twitch with renewed excitement. "Do you want me to help you get dressed?"

Blood surged down my cock at the same time Bailey made a noise in the back of his throat that sounded anything but happy.

I glared at him. "What's your issue? You can't possibly be jealous." I struggled to stay kneeling, feeling at a complete disadvantage as Bailey towered over me.

"Why?" Bailey rasped, sounding like he'd swallowed glass.

"Because I offered you my fucking heart on a platter and you all but threw it back in my fucking face," I shouted, spittle flying from my mouth, but I was too angry to care as memories of that day merged with the here and now. "I came to you to tell you how I felt, how I'd felt for years. It took me fucking months to build up the courage to come and face what was between us."

"There—"

"Don't you fucking dare deny there was anything between us, you fucking coward. I'm not blind. I could see it every time you looked at me. It was the same look I'd seen in the mirror reflected back at me daily. Those few times you allowed yourself to touch me, I felt it."

Tears ran unchecked down my cheeks as the raw emotions from that day continued to surge through me, leaving me no place to hide. "I love you. God, I love you so much I couldn't breathe for it. Then you cast me aside like I was last week's dirty washing, like I meant absolutely nothing to you. So you have no right to judge me. To criticize me for moving on or for looking for someone that might be interested in more with...someone like me." I choked out the last part, struggling to see through the tears.

Strong arms wrapped around me and I was bodily lifted off the floor. Jake's scent surrounded me as I buried my face into his neck and clung on unashamedly. "I've got you, Sam," he muttered into my hair as he sat and tucked my body into his. The fact my legs were curled up against his body barely registered with everything else going on inside my head.

My head felt like it was stuffed with cotton wool when I finally felt able to lift my face and wipe at my wet cheeks. I sniffed and blinked my eyes into focus. Bailey remained rooted to the same spot, his face a mask of desolation that I wanted to say didn't hurt my heart, but I'd never lied to myself before so I accepted the pain it caused. A part that wasn't ready to forgive right then, ignored the part that understood that Bailey had suffered too. It was there on his face, etched into the tiny lines around his eyes and pinched mouth.

Would I ever be able to look at him and not love him with my whole heart?

I sighed in defeat and shut my eyes to shield my feelings that were too close to the surface right then. I felt bruised and battered and didn't feel able to take any more hits. Only, I got a feeling in my gut that there was more to come when one of these men finally got around to telling me what Bailey was doing here.

The tension in the room grew, but I kept my eyes closed and waited.

"Sam. Sam, look at me?" Jake requested gently but firmly.

I blinked open my eyes and stared up at his face, my breath stilling in my chest.

"Bailey lives with me," he paused as I went to move, and his arms tightened around me.

"As my tenant," he stressed. "Nathan asked if I'd rent a room to Bailey when he decided to come to London."

As he finished talking, I stopped trying to get up and swallowed past the ball in my throat. I didn't look at Bailey. I couldn't right then, so I kept my gaze on Jake. "He's your tenant and nothing more?"

His brow quirked up and he got a strange look on his face. "Up till now, he's only been my tenant." He shifted his gaze to Bailey then back to me. "But I'll be honest, I want more."

The sound of Bailey sucking in a breath caused my heart to sink, right along with any hopes I'd harboured about either man wanting me too.

"I want more with the two of you," Jake continued calmly.

There was another loud exhale, but I was too busy recalling the vivid image of me sandwiched between these two men to give it too much thought. "Both of us?" The flare of hope wouldn't be denied as I gave a furtive look in Bailey's direction.

His head hung and I couldn't see his expression, but his heaving chest said he wasn't as unaffected by the idea. Then the ache in my heart reminded me that he'd already rejected me. That the cotton-wool feeling in my head was from yet more tears I'd spilled over him.

As if Jake had read my thoughts, he cupped my cheek. "I was hoping that when you arrived this morning we could have talked—"

"There wasn't much talking going on that I could see," Bailey growled, his gaze no longer fixed on the floor but on me and Jake.

He radiated the dominance that I was used to seeing in his role as a sergeant, that had hidden his true nature, and I shuddered in Jake's lap. He looked anything but pleased as deep furrows appeared in his forehead.

Jake stroked my naked back before shifting my weight onto the cushion as he rose. He gave me a gentle smile before he turned his attention to Bailey, his face becoming a dominant mask.

My cock stiffened from the aura of dominance Jake threw off as he stalked towards Bailey.

The air got stuck in my chest as Jake, though younger, shorter, and not as broad as Bailey, held Bailey's stare with powerful confidence that thickened the air surrounding them with palpable tension.

I could barely swallow, and I swear I didn't blink for fear I might miss a second of this battle of wills.

"Who is the Dom here?" Jake asked with quiet authority.

Fuck! I pushed my hand down against my cock and willed it to behave as it thrummed from the exchange. I could see the war that Bailey fought with himself as he continued to meet Jake's stare. His whole body was rigid with tension, his hands balled into fists at his sides. The seconds ticked by, and it was as if both men forgot I was in the room as they vied for dominance. There was one distinct difference between them, one was so much more confident than the other.

How had I not seen this before? How had I not noticed that Bailey's dominance was all show? This wasn't who he was, not really. Was this why he'd rejected me? Because we're too alike? As the idea took root, it distracted me enough that it took a second to register that Bailey had spun around and was yet again walking away.

Bloodyshittinghell! What was it with him and leaving?

CHAPTER FIFTEEN

JAKE

The air rushed out of my chest at Bailey's retreating back. I'd not missed the fleeting look of regret as he'd turned to leave. I held on to the hope that he just needed time to think now I'd challenged him to face who he was and what he wanted.

What if that's just Sam? *Then I'd deal with that...and show him he was wrong.* I'd worked towards all my life goals with determination and an unwavering vision. After the conversation with Nathan, I'd created a new vision for my personal life and it now contained these two men. And Bailey was going to have to get used to it.

Mal, the Dom who'd trained me, had taught me well. And if there was one thing I was good at besides architecture, it was being a Dom.

"He left...again." The sobbed cry from Sam brought my attention back to him.

I was across the room and lifting him back into my lap in a heartbeat. He came willingly, even as he stared at the empty doorway with such longing, it cut me to the bone. Wrapping my arms around him, it took a second to register how cool his skin felt. I tugged him closer to me and rubbed at his pebbled flesh.

"I don't think I can keep doing this," Sam cried, burying his face into my neck. His tears dampened my skin as he wept.

"Hey. Hey now. Come on, enough, Sam. I want you to listen to me." I waited till he glanced up at me with tear-drenched eyes, then wiped at the tears running down his cheeks. "I've no intention of letting him go. The same applies to you."

His breath hitched and he blinked rapidly. "What if you're left with just me?" he whispered as if afraid to give voice to his fear.

I met his gaze, seeing how much it cost him to ask. I cupped his pale cheeks. "As an architect, I've learned many lessons about having to change my plans to make them work to fit a new dynamic."

His lower lip poked out in an adorable pout which I found irresistible, so I laid a gentle kiss on his lips. "With or without Bailey, I want to carry on seeing you. That won't change. You've been honest about how you feel for Bailey, so I feel I'm ahead of the game. I won't ask yet if you've got room enough in your heart for someone else, it's too soon. But know this, that is what I'm aiming for."

He sucked in a watery breath, releasing it on a shuddery exhale.

"I didn't lie to Bailey, I'd every intention of talking to you both this morning about trying to figure out whether you'd both like me to be your Dom. Only, he never came home, and I didn't know where he was. I've given a lot of thought since Saturday about what I want. About what I could offer to you, and to Bailey if he'll let me. I think I could be the missing piece that connects you to Bailey, and Bailey to you and me."

Sam started to wriggle in my lap, distracting me. I glanced down, immediately figuring out why. The cock that had lost its arousal during the fight with Bailey now stood proud from his groin, the tip coated with pre-cum.

My own body reacted to the sight and he squirmed anew as my cock pressed up against his arse. I held him still. "I can clearly see you like my idea, but understand this, if you decide that this is what you want with me, with Bailey, then we need to wait for Bailey before anything more happens. He's right. There wasn't much talking as I got ahead of myself when you arrived earlier. You're far too tempting." I flicked a finger down his nose as he huffed but nodded.

"What...what if he only wants me?"

"Then I'll tie him up to my St. Andrew's Cross until he sees sense," I growled, knowing damn well I meant every word.

I'd seen in Bailey's eyes how much he wanted what I could give him, what Sam could give him. He was scared, and it was up to me to show him he could let go and find that place, that part of his soul he was missing, his submission.

Sam snuggled into my chest. "Can I watch when you do that? I have a feeling you're gonna have a battle on your hands." He sounded a little fatalistic, but then he'd already experienced

Bailey's stubborn nature and had suffered the consequences.

"I'll not only let you watch, Pup, I'll let you play too."

Sam gasped and jerked to a sitting position, his face showing too many emotions to figure out if I'd said something wrong.

"What is it?" I asked, finding it hard to keep my voice even as my heart raced.

"You'll let me join in, with you and Bailey? I'll not just be sitting watching?"

I chuckled as relief poured through me. "Sam, this is about the three of us. We'll figure out what works, but it's my intention to make sure no one feels excluded. But just an FYI, watching can be a lot of fun."

He fidgeted against me and I groaned as he moaned and pushed down on his cock.

I took a firm but gentle hold of his wrist and lifted it away from his groin. "That won't do. That pretty cock is mine, and there'll be no touching unless I say."

His eyes widened before they looked towards the open door. "Then you'll need to work faster with Bailey because I'm not sure how long I can hold off," he all but whined, his face pinching in distress as he glanced at his lap.

I murmured in his ear, "Think about all the rewards I'll give you for being a good Pup."

"Oh god!" He groaned as his legs clamped together. "That was so unfair."

"Yes, I know, but remember, I'll be in the same position as you. I won't touch myself until I can do it in front of you and Bailey."

He panted and the leg squeezing increased as his hands came up and grabbed hold of my top. "Fuck, you fight dirty," he groaned.

I laughed as exhilaration I'd not felt in too long to remember surfaced, and I gave Sam an evil grin. "You don't know the half of it. And I can't wait to show you and Bailey."

For the exciting conclusion click here....

OTHER BOOKS

Standalone
When Fake Changed Everything
Christmas beyond Christmas
The Elves and the Bondage Daddy (Grim and
Sinister Delights Book 5)

Series
The Potters Creek Series
A Christmas Wish (book one)

The App Series
The App: Daddy kink (book one)
The App: Littles (book two)
The App: Puppy play (book three)

The Flamingo Bar Series
Always More (book one)
The Little Side of Me (book two)
3 is the magic number (book three) - **Feb 2021**

La Trattoria Di Amore Series
Puzzle Pieces (book one)
Dominated but not Subdued (book two)

The Playroom Series
Mine, Body and Soul: Part One
Mine, Body and Soul: Part Two
Mine, Body and Soul: Part Three
Ferron's Journey: Damaged Part One (book four)
Ferron's Journey: Hidden Part Two (book five)
Ferron's Journey: Revelation Part Three (book six)
Mine, Body and Soul Trilogy
Ferron's Journey Trilogy

Dark River Stone Collective Series
The light beneath the dark

The Billionaire Playground Series
Property of a Billionaire (Book one)
Reluctant Billionaire (Book two)

The Manx Cat Guardians Series
Where it all Began: Origins (Book 1)
Seeing Beyond the Scars (Book 2)
Destiny Collides Past and Present (Book 3)
Searching for a Soul to Love (Book 4)
The 12 Disasters of Christmas (Book 5)
Laws of Attraction (Book 6)
The Teacher's Boy (Book 7)
Boxset

Audio Books

Mine, Body and Soul, Part One: The Playroom Series
Mine, Body and Soul, Part Two: The Playroom Series
Mine, Body and Soul, Part Three: The Playroom Series
Daddy Kink: The App (book one)
Always More: The Flamingo Bar (book one)
When Fake Changed Everything
Ferron's Journey: Damaged Part One

ABOUT THE AUTHOR

Hi all,

My name is Jayne and I live in the Isle of Man. A tiny place in the Irish sea. It's an island steeped in folklore and history and just begs to have stories written about it, and one of my true inspirations.

I've been happily married for over 25 years to a wonderfully complicated man, and I have a wonderful daughter with two very young grandbabies. I am also an identical twin, so if you see me, check, as it may not be me.

I've written an eclectic mix of books, mainly contemporary gay romance with a paranormal twist, daddy kink, fake boyfriends, out for you and enemies to lovers, along with many other tropes. All of my series are listed if you want to find other books to read. They are all on Amazon and in KU.

If you're interested in keeping up to date with what I'm planning then why don't you follow and join me on the following links.

You can find me and follow me on:

Newsletter Sign up

Goodreads

Tumblr

Bookbub

Instagram

Twitter

Facebook

Website address

Facebook Author page

JP Manx Minx's

If you would like to give me any feedback or just have any questions, go ahead and friend me on Facebook, and I would be happy to answer anything. Well, almost anything. I hope you enjoyed this book as it was a little different for me. If you would also like to leave a review, then I would love to read your thoughts.

Thank you for taking the time to be part of my dream.